P9-DEI-292

FRIEND IN NEED

Lily Sly was Les Coyle's woman, and Les was Ruff Justice's friend. But a bullet in the night had put Les out of action, and left Ruff and the lovely blonde Lily together.

Still, Ruff could hardly believe his suddenly aroused senses when he was woken as he slept on the floor. He saw Lily standing in front of the firelight, her voluptuous body plainly outlined in the thin nightgown she wore. Then he felt her hand slip under his blanket in search of his warmth.

"I'm afraid," she murmured, her cheek against his thigh now. "Afraid and lonely. Don't make me be alone." She looked up, her hand gripping him.

"Lily," he said, "it's no good this way."

"It is good," she said.

And the way she went about proving it, Ruff couldn't argue anymore. . . .

Wild Westerns by Warren T. Longtree

(0451)

☐ RUFF JUSTICE #1: SUDDEN THUNDER (110285—$2.50)
☐ RUFF JUSTICE #2: NIGHT OF THE APACHE (110293—$2.50)
☐ RUFF JUSTICE #3: BLOOD ON THE MOON (112256—$2.50)
☐ RUFF JUSTICE #4: WIDOW CREEK (114221—$2.50)
☐ RUFF JUSTICE #5: VALLEY OF GOLDEN TOMBS (115635—$2.50)
☐ RUFF JUSTICE #6: THE SPIRIT WOMAN WAR (117832—$2.50)
☐ RUFF JUSTICE #7: DARK ANGEL RIDING (118820—$2.50)
☐ RUFF JUSTICE #8: THE DEATH OF IRON HORSE (121449—$2.50)
☐ RUFF JUSTICE #9: WINDWOLF (122828—$2.50)
☐ RUFF JUSTICE #10: SHOSHONE RUN (123883—$2.50)
☐ RUFF JUSTICE #11: COMANCHE PEAK (124901—$2.50)
☐ RUFF JUSTICE #12: PETTICOAT EXPRESS (127765—$2.50)
☐ RUFF JUSTICE #13: POWER LODE (128788—$2.50)
☐ RUFF JUSTICE #14: THE STONE WARRIORS (129733—$2.50)
☐ RUFF JUSTICE #15: CHEYENNE MOON (131177—$2.50)
☐ RUFF JUSTICE #16: HIGH VENGEANCE (132009—$2.50)
☐ RUFF JUSTICE #17: DRUM ROLL (132815—$2.50)
☐ RUFF JUSTICE #18: THE RIVERBOAT QUEEN (134125—$2.50)
☐ RUFF JUSTICE #19: FRENCHMAN'S PASS (135288—$2.50)
☐ RUFF JUSTICE #20: THE SONORA BADMAN (136233—$2.75)
☐ RUFF JUSTICE #21: THE DENVER DUCHESS (137752—$2.75)

*Price is higher in Canada

Buy them at your local bookstore or use this convenient coupon for ordering.

NEW AMERICAN LIBRARY,
P.O. Box 999, Bergenfield, New Jersey 07621

Please send me the books I have checked above. I am enclosing $_____
(please add $1.00 to this order to cover postage and handling). Send check
or money order—no cash or C.O.D.'s. Prices and numbers are subject to change
without notice.

Name_____

Address_____

City_____ State_____ Zip Code_____
Allow 4-6 weeks for delivery.
This offer is subject to withdrawal without notice.

RUFF JUSTICE #21

The Denver Duchess

by
Warren T. Longtree

A SIGNET BOOK

NEW AMERICAN LIBRARY

PUBLISHER'S NOTE

This novel is a work of fiction. Names, characters, places, and incidents either are the product of the author's imagination or are used fictitiously, and any resemblance to actual persons, living or dead, events, or locales is entirely coincidental.

NAL BOOKS ARE AVAILABLE AT QUANTITY DISCOUNTS WHEN USED TO PROMOTE PRODUCTS OR SERVICES. FOR INFORMATION PLEASE WRITE TO PREMIUM MARKETING DIVISION, NEW AMERICAN LIBRARY, 1633 BROADWAY, NEW YORK, NEW YORK 10019.

Copyright © 1985 by New American Library

All rights reserved

The first chapter of this book appeared in *The Sonora Badman*, the twentieth volume of this series.

SIGNET TRADEMARK REG. U.S. PAT. OFF. AND FOREIGN COUNTRIES
REGISTERED TRADEMARK—MARCA REGISTRADA
HECHO EN CHICAGO, U.S.A.

SIGNET, SIGNET CLASSIC, MENTOR, PLUME, MERIDIAN AND NAL BOOKS are published by New American Library, 1633 Broadway, New York, New York 10019

First Printing, August, 1985

1 2 3 4 5 6 7 8 9

PRINTED IN THE UNITED STATES OF AMERICA

RUFF JUSTICE

He knew the West better than any man alive—a hostile, savage land rife with both violent outlaws and courageous adventurers. But Ruff Justice had a sixth sense that kept him breathing and saw his enemies dead. A scout for the U.S. Cavalry, he was paid to protect the public, and nobody was faster at sniffing out a killer, a crook, a con man—red or white, at close range or far. Anyone on the wrong side of the law would have to reckon with the menace of Ruff's murderously sharp stag-handled bowie knife, with his Colt pistol, and the Spencer rifle he cradled in his arms.

Ruff Justice, gentleman and frontier philospher—good men respected him, bad men feared him, and women, good and bad, wanted him with all the wildness of the Old West.

1

The tall man, dressed in buckskins, stepped from the railroad car onto the station platform. He had a satchel in one hand and a .56-caliber Spencer repeating rifle in the other. He took in slow, deep breaths of the cool, clean air. The sign on the depot eaves read: DENVER, COLORADO ALT. 5,280 FT.

Lifting his eyes, the tall man could see the peaks of the high mountains, the Rockies, stretching their grandeur skyward. Massive and sprawling, they were beautiful, raw, and just a little intimidating.

"Ruffin!" a voice called out.

The tall man turned his head toward the voice, which belonged to a reedy blond man in a sheepskin coat. There was a badge pinned to his blue flannel shirt.

Ruff Justice put down his bag and rifle and stuck out a hand, which the other man took warmly.

"How's everything, Les?"

"Fine, Ruffin. Just fine." He still held Ruff's hand. The two men stood looking at each other, assuring themselves that an old friend still walked the earth despite the hazards of life. "I couldn't believe it when I got your wire. I would have thought you were buzzard bait long ago."

"They keep trying," Justice answered with a smile. "Still town marshal, I see. They haven't squeezed you out yet."

Les Coyle smiled thinly. "They keep trying, Ruff. They keep trying." Then he slapped Justice on the shoulder and said, "Come on uptown. We can walk. You want to stay at the jailhouse or are you flush enough for the Grand Hotel?"

"The army still pays me," Justice told Coyle. "I'll try the Grand again. They still got running water or did that experiment bust?"

"They've got it," the marshal said. "The damn holding tank busted last winter, sheeting the front of the hotel with ice, but they've got it all back together now. I hear the place across the street is going to try it as well. Next thing you know there'll be running water everywhere."

Denver hadn't changed, and yet it was greatly different, Justice thought. It still bustled, hustled, built up and tore down; you could still see drunks and whores on the streets at nine in the morning, find a cutthroat to do a quick midnight job for you, lose a fortune at faro or win a year's wages on the spin of a wheel; the gold mines were still turning out enormous profits for the lucky few, becoming slave pits for the many, and financial heartbreakers for some. Denver was still the richest city between the Mississippi and San Francisco. The overnighters, the miners who found themselves sitting on top of a mountain of gold ore and hadn't an idea in the world of how to spend it, were still building their mansions on the outskirts of town, touring Europe to loot it of art objects and its veneer of culture, and coming home even richer and only a little wiser.

Yet it had changed. The old Amory House had been burned down by an arsonist angry at the loss of his stake in a poker game. Wichita Charley, who used to roam the streets in a bearskin and ten-gallon hat—winter or summer—had been killed by an unknown person with no sense of humor or tolerance. They had paved a section of Central Avenue with red bricks; Hadley's tent-town mercantile had gone from canvas to frame and clapboard. There were a hell of a lot more people.

"I've got seven deputies," Les Coyle told Justice, "and that's not half enough. If you ever want a job wearing a badge . . ."

"No, thank you! I've got enough trouble in my life," Ruff said with a smile.

"I hear you look for half of it."

"Maybe. It kind of careens toward me, though."

"Ruff . . ." Les Coyle stopped, smiled boyishly, and scratched his arm. "I'm gettin' married."

"Well, damn me. You don't mean it."

"I do," Coyle said hastily. Then he grew meditative. "You don't think . . . I'm a lawman, Ruff . . . Some folks say it's wrong for a lawman to marry and have kids. You know how it gets in these towns when the midnight fever strikes. Every man on the street's got a gun, and every other one wants to plug me for one reason or the other."

"You're asking me what to do?" Ruff laughed. "Hell, Les, you must want her. She must want you. She knows what you do for a living. Don't let other people do your thinking for you. You two know what's best."

"Yeah. It's just—"

"It'll hurt her as much, maybe more, if you were never man and wife—if and when it happens. Christ, look at you. You must be old enough to go on pension now anyway! You can't have many working years left."

"I'm a year older than you, Ruffin T. Justice, and you

know it. Those are worry lines on my face, something you wouldn't know about."

They started up Bond Street, crossed the road at the Cassio Brothers Store, climbed the steps, and entered the marshal's office, which was situated above the store.

Ruff looked around, nodded, put his bag down, and tossed his hat on the desk. "Home?" he asked.

"For now. We've got a little place outside of town—back near Colson Canyon. Lily's still fixing it up." Coyle hung his head sheepishly. "You know, yellow curtains and such."

Ruff had been reading the wanted posters on the wall. Now he plopped himself into Les Coyle's swivel chair. "When do I get to meet her?"

"Tonight. If you want to. I didn't—"

"Come on, Les. What do you think I want to do? Of course I want to meet her. Give you my approval and all."

"Maybe I'm afraid to let you near her," Coyle joked.

"Maybe you should be. Tonight?"

"Sure . . . Well, why don't you go with us?" the marshal said, brightening.

"Go with you where?" Ruff asked.

"To the ball. All of Denver's going. I even got an invite. Not because of me, but because Lily knows all those folks, you see. Her mother was some kind of cousin removed."

"Les, you know I have no idea what you're talking about, don't you? As for any kind of ball, what I had in mind was a peaceful night at the Grand—a hot bath, a meal, a soft pillow." All of which would be a great change from sleeping out on the Mexican desert, living off roots and dried venison, which was what Justice had been doing for the past few weeks before stepping on that northbound train and heading for Dakota. He had decided to spend a few days in Denver to get warm and spoiled and to look up a few old friends like Les Coyle. He was ready for some of that warmth and spoiling now. Not for some fancy-dress ball.

"The Duchess is staging this thing, Ruff. In a way it's kind of an engagement party for me and Lily. Duchess Duchamp-Villon." Coyle chuckled. "The former Katie Price."

"Didn't she work at the Scottish Wheel?"

"The same. But she didn't *work* there, Ruff; she owned it. Yes, our Katie was something even then, beautiful and well-off, huh? But when this Duke Duchamp-Villon came over here to buy the Never-Never Mine from Willy McDowell and the Ute—"

"They sold out?" Ruff interrupted, surprised at the news.

"Yes, just before the Never-Never opened up onto a vein six yards wide of jewelers'-grade gold. Well, McDowell got so mad he drank himself to death. The Ute spent all of his take on cloth and beads and trade knives and then went back to the mountains to live like a king among his own people."

"And the Frenchman got wealthy?"

"Well, he already was, you see. He worked for some sort of cartel, but he had a stake in it too. Yes, he got rich. And then he got lonely, and then he got Katie Price out of the Scottish Wheel, and then he got killed."

"Here?"

"Right here. After he and Katie got back from a six-month honeymoon in Europe. Now the Duchess is *very* rich. She's got a three-story stone house on Gower, with gold fixtures in the bathrooms—twelve of them! And you think the men around here don't chase her? Good Lord! But she's not high-toned around folks, Ruffin. She knows that, underneath, she's still Katie Price. So she gives a

11

costume ball like this, and she invites all her old friends as well as the upper crust."

"A costume ball. Now I know I'm not going."

"Not even to meet Lily?"

"No."

"Or for a chance to see our Denver Duchess up close?"

"No."

"Not for anything in the world, even though I've got a costume made up for you and everything?" a soft female voice asked.

The second voice came from behind Justice. It was pearly and gentle as velvet, inviting and feminine, and Ruff turned slowly to its summons.

"Please?"

She was tall, her dark hair stacked and curled beneath a tiny hat. Her figure was lush and undeniable beneath the black silk that was draped lovingly over her body. Her lips were full; her nose softly arched, nostrils flaring; and when she smiled, she revealed even white teeth. Her green eyes sparkled with the invitation that the tilt and thrust of her hips seemed to imply.

"I'm not used to being refused," the Duchess Duchamp-Villon said to Ruff Justice. "I'd like you to come to the ball. I'm in mourning, but I could offer you a dance."

It seemed she was offering much more than that. Justice glanced at Les, and damn him, he was smiling. The marshal knew that Justice wasn't the kind to turn down an invitation like this one. And he was dead right.

"Tonight, then," Justice said, bowing from the neck.

"Tonight," the Duchess of Denver said. "Yes, I believe it will be tonight."

12

2

His name was Ruff Justice. He was tall and lean with cold blue eyes, eyes that had seen many things savage and beautiful, bloody and incredible in his years in the wild country. He had made a few friends, good friends like Les Coyle, and uncounted enemies, some of whom no longer walked the earth.

He had been called every name a reasonably fluent English-speaking American could conjure up, and he had been called some in other languages, too—among them scoundrel and pirate, but he had never looked more like a pirate then he did that night.

He stood before the mahogany-encased oval mirror and looked at his bluish reflection. Long dark hair curled past his shoulders; a black mustache drooped to his jawline, curving slightly outward. On his head was a red bandanna, and over one eye was a black patch. He also wore a red sash around his narrow waist and a blue silk shirt. He felt just a little foolish, but if this was the way they did things in Denver, it was all right with Ruffin T. Justice.

The knock on the hotel-room door turned his head, and out of habit Ruff reached for the long-barreled .44 caliber Colt Peacemaker, that rested on the bureau before him.

"Come in," Ruff said.

It was Les Coyle, smiling with delight, quietly noting the big revolver. The town marshal was in costume as well, wearing a cavalier's outfit with a broad belt that held a rapier running from shoulder to opposite hip, and a plumed broad hat. In his hand was a mask.

"Well, you look the part," Coyle said.

"Whose idea was this—the pirate part?" Ruff asked with a grin. "I see myself more as a cavalier."

"I did my best." Coyle sat in a wooden chair, examining Ruff critically. "Yeah, that's the right outfit for you."

"It's a wonder you didn't make me up as an executioner or such."

"That costume was gone," Les said with mock regret. "The ladies will love it. Rugged and adventurous."

"Sure," Ruff mumbled, putting his .44 away, and from the bureau drawer he withdrew his little Colt New Line .41 and slipped it into a shoulder holster beneath his silk shirt.

Les Coyle frowned. "Ruff, you don't need anything like that."

"No? I've been caught without one, Les, and I didn't like it a bit. You ought to know that better than anyone else, considering the line of work you're in."

"Ruff," Coyle said, rising, "at the Duchess's costume ball? You positively won't need that. Maybe down on Delaney Street, now . . ."

"It's a good-luck charm, let's leave it at that."

They had been friends too long to argue about it, too long for Les Coyle to think he could talk Ruff Justice out of doing anything he had set his mind on doing.

Outside, it was cold and clear. From uptown drifted the sounds of the renewable nightly brawl: glass breaking, someone owl-hooting, a woman screaming.

Les Coyle stopped and looked that way, shaking his head.

"Your deputies will stop it, Les," Ruff assured him.

"I know. I just feel bad going to a fancy ball and leaving Jody or Ty to get cut up or shot."

"That's what they hired on for."

"Yes. Me too."

A buggy with a liveried driver was waiting for them. Ruff, feeling as foolish as Coyle seemed to, stepped up and seated himself, careful of his toy sword. The driver snapped the reins and the marshal of Denver and his guest were driven from town.

"Not down Grand Street, damn all!" Coyle said to the driver, and the man, who seemed to be smiling, turned up a side road. "It wouldn't do me much good to be seen cavorting around in a plumed hat, toting a sword," Coyle growled.

They passed a low, dark bar that seemed to emit the stench of depravity and death. "That's Chase Longden's place. The next bar there, on the left, belongs to Blue Boy Weaver."

"I thought you locked them up a long while back," Ruff commented.

Justice remembered the names. Longden had been the brains, Blue Boy the muscle of an extortion ring that had branched out to include every vice and crime Denver had to offer, though extortion had remained their prime concern.

"I had them arrested and they were sentenced. But, Ruff, you'd be surprised how few witnesses I could find by the second day of the trial. Mac Magoon was the first witness the first day. That night we found old Mac with

15

both of his arms broken. He said a wagon ran over him. The next day there wasn't a single witness to be found. I should have locked the batch of them up. On the strength of Mac's testimony Chase and Blue Boy got six months each. They're out now, though, better-off than ever."

"How do they stand with you?" Ruff asked.

"Well, they promised to kill me, of course, but every other thug in Denver has promised that. If you let such stuff bother you, you're in the wrong business. There's the house," he said, pointing. "Now tell me what you think of that, Ruffin!"

The house of the Duchess of Denver sat on a small, landscaped knoll, surrounded by a wrought-iron fence supported by brick pillars. The house was also brick, three and a half stories tall. Light blazed from every window. Surreys and buggies stood before the structure on a long gravel driveway, its entrance guarded by two stone lions. A green lawn, two to three acres of it, wrapped around the knoll. Although winter was coming on, the grass was alive and flourishing.

Ruff could hear an orchestra playing, could see ladies in ball gowns and masks being helped from buggies and up the steps to the entranceway, which was smothered in jasmine and French ivy. On the broad lawn, magnolia trees, magically in blossom despite the cold, gave off their rich scent. The upstairs balconies were done in wrought iron, reminiscent of the French Quarter in New Orleans.

It had taken money to build the house, and money to maintain it—and plenty of it. But then they said the Duchess was loaded. Her murdered husband had left her plenty, enough so that it wouldn't run out no matter how hard she tried to spend it. She had twelve indoor bathrooms; she could have had a hundred. The Never-

Never Mine was famed far and wide. It straddled the Mother Lode, and if there was an end to its wealth, it hadn't been reached yet.

The two men stepped from the coach, feeling slightly less foolish, now that they were surrounded by other men in costume, other ladies in ball gowns and masks. There were clowns and devils and convicts inside the house, as well as kings, Napoleons, George Washingtons, and minstrels.

And across the room stood Les Coyle's woman, this Lily who had taken a good, hard town marshal and made him go all round-eyed and ready to settle down into a little white house with yellow curtains.

"Come on," Coyle said, leading Ruff, whose piratical good looks drew a glance from more than one lady. They crossed the entire length of the ballroom, which was bigger than most houses, chandelier-lit, and hung with bunting. Denver's finest stood in groups, the whiskered men, who were heavy with good fortune, smoked cigars; their women, often younger, purchased with gold, were demure or bold or cunning. Here and there a dowager, more knowing than any of them, decided how to consolidate her important social position: who to scorn, who to associate with, who to besiege.

"This," Les Coyle said with glowing pride as they stopped before the pert little blonde in blue, "is Miss Lily Sly."

The name didn't fit her. She was girlishly plump, her round face faintly freckled under a dusting of face powder, her body all cream and apples and young, unformed sexuality. It seemed Les had found him a virgin queen, a healthy, happy helpmate.

"I'm pleased to meet you," Ruff said, bowing slightly. He took her hand and kissed it gently, quickly. He then smiled and patted her hand. "Les is my good friend. I hope we'll be friends as well."

"I know we will be," Lily Sly said with a full smile. It was the smile of a happy youth, not the inviting, coy smile of other women Ruff had encountered. She was Les' woman, and she saved those smiles for him. "I've heard so much about you," Lily added, cocking her head and looking at him with a kind of wonder in her pale-gray eyes. "I can hardly believe it's all true."

"It isn't," Justice said.

"I don't know if that's modesty or shame," Les Coyle said. "It might not all be true, but I've seen a lot of it myself."

"Let's skip around that stuff," Ruff requested. "We've all done some things we wouldn't care to hear repeated."

"But few of us have done so many." Coyle laughed.

A new voice, soft and flirtatious, but of deep and exotic tones, put in, "Such as?"

They turned to find the Duchess standing behind them. Ruff Justice lifted an eyebrow. The lady was in white satin. The dress flowed down across her breasts, revealing much but promising even more. It cinched around her narrow waist and then flared out again over her fascinating, compelling hips.

"What sorts of things has Mister Justice done?" the Duchess asked, and she managed to move closer to Ruff so that she was only inches from him, looking up. The light from the crystal chandeliers danced in her eyes and in the diamonds she wore around her throat, diamonds in constellation, ostentatious on anyone else but seeming quite at home, nestled between the Duchess's sleek pale throat and her smoothly rounded cleavage.

"I've been in the West a long while," Justice said. "I've had the sort of trouble any man out here has."

Coyle laughed. "Yes, he has, and he's the only one I

know who has managed to survive it all and to enjoy it to the hilt. He's the only man I know who has traveled to Europe with Bill Cody to read his poetry before the royalty. The only man who has managed to make a legend of himself *and* stay alive in the service of the U.S. Army."

"Easy, Les, I'm getting embarrassed."

"That would be the day." Les laughed. "The man hasn't got emotions—not of that sort anyway."

"No?" Denver's Duchess asked. "What kind of emotions *does* Mister Ruffin T. Justice have?"

Ruff, who was captivated by the green eyes and the soft, deep voice of the woman before him, was saved an answer by the rumble of the orchestra.

"Would you care to dance?" he asked, and the Duchess's eyes softened. There seemed to be a laugh behind them waiting to burst forth, but it was restrained now. The Duchess Duchamp-Villon held out a white-gloved hand, and Ruff Justice took it.

On the dance floor they began to make the grand turn and cross the walnut floor as the other dancers— Denver's mining kings and politicians and newly tamed and curried citizens of various wild and sometimes unsavory backgrounds—followed awkwardly.

"Damn your eyes, Ruff Justice," the Duchess of Denver said, and no one saw her lean forward and bite his neck.

"Katie Price, you're a hard woman," Ruff answered, laughing out loud so that heads turned toward them as they swirled across the floor.

"Why didn't you tell me you were coming back?"

"Why didn't you tell me you were a duchess of what-not?"

"How would I do that? When's the last time I saw you, Ruff, and who the hell ever knows where you're going to be next?"

The spirit was light, but there was a serious undertone to her words. Ruff knew Katie Price—oh, yes, he knew her. They had been more than friends and, during one long winter they had almost become more than lovers. But Justice had had a job to complete, and Katie had wanted more than to wait and watch a door that never opened.

"Bastard," she whispered softly, and they danced on.

Les Coyle, who hadn't known about their past, stared in amazement as they swirled by. He was dancing with Lily, the only woman he cared for in all of Denver. In something close to awe he watched Ruff, watched the expression on the Duchess's face, and said, "I told you he was fast, but damn me, I've never seen a thing quite like that."

They continued to dance, Les still amazed, glancing at his friend from time to time. Around them the costumed figures darted and moved in a haze of champagne. The Duchess was free with her hospitality, and the men of Denver were free in their acceptance of it. One noted citizen had already reached the point of excess and had been quietly escorted out the back way.

"Marshal?"

Coyle stopped and looked at the masked imp who held up a note for him.

"Yes, what is it?" Les frowned. Trouble tonight? He didn't need it; yet it was far from unexpected. Denver was like a caldron, always ready to simmer over.

"Man gave me this note, sir," the kid said, thrusting the paper into Coyle's hand and then scooting away through the dancers.

"What is it, Les?" Lily asked.

"I've no idea," Coyle told her. The note wasn't very specific:

Marshal,

We got to talk. Come to the summerhouse. There's something you ought to know about.

Les Coyle showed it to Lily and she studied it, her lips moving unhappily, her eyes bright and wondering. She gave the note back and shook her head.

"You can't go."

"I have to, don't I?" the man in the cavalier costume responded.

"Why?"

"Because someone thinks something is important enough to tell me. Important enough to contact me in the middle of the Duchess's fancy ball."

"Les, darn all!" Lily was exasperated. "You know as well as I do that it might be a trap."

"A trap? Who would want to set a trap for me? My friends wouldn't, and my enemies are the kind to walk up and spit in my eye while they're shooting me." Les laughed, but Lily only shook her head, not liking a bit of it. He kissed her and then turned away, leaving her to walk to the punch bowl and unhappily sip the deep wine-red punch, which smelled suspiciously of rum.

Ruff Justice finished the dance with the Duchess and they turned to applaud the orchestra briefly. The next song was struck up and the movement began again.

"Another dance?" Ruff asked.

"Take me outside."

"What about your duties? You are the hostess, aren't you?"

"Hostess be damned. I'm Katie Price, and a man I care for has come home."

"For a little while."

"Well, maybe that's long enough."

Ruff didn't argue with the lady. They made their way

21

toward the patio door, the Duchess with all the skills of a polished hostess, brushing off the people in their way as if she were welcoming them, as if her greatest regret was that she couldn't spend all evening with each and every one of them.

They reached the glass-paned door, which was opened by a man in a dark suit who bowed to the Duchess, and passed through. It was cold outside, the stars brittle and bright in a black sky. The oak trees cut grotesque figures against the night, the stars winking through the lace of their foliage. The Duchess moved into Ruff's arms, and she was warm and sweet, her parted lips insistent as she clung to Justice, her body sagging against his.

Justice kissed her and drew her nearer. The night was cold, too cold. Inside, the dancers in costumes and ball gowns flowed past the lighted window. The Duchess rested her head against his chest and whispered, "Oh, God, Justice, how I've missed you."

"You look like you've been lonely," he teased.

"This? Other nights like it? Mobs of people? Things like that don't mean anything, and you know it. Not when you're missing someone, wanting something you can't find anywhere else."

"It's been a long time, Katie."

"Meaning?" She drew back and looked up at him with star-bright eyes.

"Meaning," he said, "that it's been a long time."

But she was still lovely, and the way her lips roamed his throat and ears, the way her hands clenched and clung to him, was all too familiar. Suddenly it didn't seem so long ago that he and Katie Price had been together.

"You could have dropped a letter," she said.

"To who? Where? I knew you had gone away, but where I didn't know. Someone said you had gotten married. I heard it was the King of England once. I could almost believe it."

"Could you? No, it wasn't the king. It was a poor old Duchamp-Villon."

"Old, was he? Probably a little withered old man?"

"He was all of forty," she said. "And in excellent shape."

"Dumpy and red-nosed."

"He wore a mustache, carried himself erect, spoke precisely and interestingly, had a bundle of money, which I took him for, and he wasn't Ruff Justice."

"But you married him."

"Hell, Ruff, you'd be surprised to know how many women get married because someone asks them. I was alone; you were gone, and who knew if you'd ever come back. And I knew damn well you weren't going to marry me even if you did come back—"

"Katie . . ."

"Don't bother, Ruffin. I know you. This very kind man with proper manners and a bag full of money came along when I was tired of being alone, tired of the Scottish Wheel, and sick to death of Delaney Street and Denver and beer and gambling men and blood on Friday night—and so I married him."

"Did you kill him later?"

"That's not funny, Ruff."

"Who did, then?"

He felt her hands slide from his back, felt her mood change as she stepped away.

"Are you carrying a badge now?"

"No. But I get curious."

"I don't know who did it. It sure wasn't me, though at the time people thought maybe it was. I had trouble with local folks and then with a battery of European lawyers . . ."

"What did they want?"

"Why, the mine, of course!"

"The Never-Never."

"That's right. Duchamp-Villon was supposed to have purchased it for the cartel he worked for, a European monopoly called Française-Froebel. But he didn't. It seems he smelled vast wealth at the Never-Never, and when Willy McDowell and the Ute signed the papers, it was solely to my husband that they sold the mine."

"He cut out his partners, his employers?"

"Apparently . . ." she hesitated. "Duchamp-Villon was a gentleman with women, but not in his business dealings."

"You think this cartel killed him?"

"I really don't know, Ruff. And I don't know if I care any longer," she admitted. "I didn't love him like . . . some women love their husbands."

"All right, let's let it drop. I'm sorry I brought it all up. I seem to have this natural curiosity to know how things were."

"How they were?" She was near him again, and she lifted his hand and placed it on her full, ripe breast. "They were lonesome, that's how things were. Lonesome and hungry and wanting."

Her lips punctuated each word as she held Ruff even closer still. Beyond her the party went on. But the Duchess of Denver seemed unaware of any of it, of anything but the tall lean man, this pirate who stood before her, his body gradually hardening as he pressed against her. He took the nape of her neck in his hand and bent to kiss her very hard, his mouth bruising hers, lifting her heartbeat to a rapid hammering.

It was then that the scream came from within the ballroom. Ruff started that way instantly, the Duchess at his heels, his hand reaching for the revolver in his shoulder holster.

Inside, Denver's finest citizens seemed to be in vast confusion. Something was happening near the bandstand, but Justice couldn't tell what it was. Then he saw the smear of blood, saw the bright colors of the cavalier's costume, and he cursed slowly, pushing his way through the mob to reach Marshal Les Coyle, who was on the floor, his bloody head on the lap of Lily Sly, his costume torn and smudged.

"What happened?" Ruff demanded.

"I don't know," Lily said, her gray eyes panicky. There was blood on the handkerchief she held in her left hand. "He'll be all right, won't he?" she asked as Ruff crouched down to examine his friend. "He'll be all right—he's got to be!"

3

Ruff Justice turned to the people gathered around him in the ballroom of the Duchess of Denver's house, and snapped angrily, "Why don't you all move back? You're not helping anything here."

By this time, Katie Price had caught up with Ruff. "What is it? What can we do, Ruff?" the Duchess asked.

"Get someone to help me carry him to a bedroom. Call for a doctor if there isn't one here, and get these people back. Either close the party down or have the band strike up something they can dance to."

As Katie turned away, the band started to play brightly. Lily Sly watched as Justice lifted the battered marshal by the shoulders, and then she said something unexpected.

"It's your fault. Your fault, Justice, for coming back. Les always said you carried trouble with you. This is all your fault."

Ruff looked at her, the single eye that was visible beneath his pirate's disguise blue and inquiring. "Sure," he said. "It's my fault."

"Sir?" A butler with heavy shoulders and a lined face that had seen more of hard weather and hot suns than of parlors and drawing rooms had appeared next to Ruff. "The Duchess requires that I—"

"Sure, Staggs, give a hoist," Ruff said, and the big man grinned.

"All right, Ruff. Kate says to take him to the first bedroom up the stairs. To the right."

Staggs had been a miner, a bouncer, and a gambler. Now he had a bad stomach and suffered from occasional dizzy spells. He was still big and powerful, and he lifted Les Coyle's feet and followed Ruff up the stairs while the bystanders parted and the band played on.

Ruff wondered briefly why Katie kept a reformed thug like Harlon Staggs around, but there wasn't much time to worry about that. Les Coyle was of greater concern. The marshal moaned as they reached the head of the stairs, and his eyes focused on Ruff.

"I'm all right. What the hell are you doing, Justice? Put me down," Les ordered.

"Shut up," Justice growled.

They found the bedroom door open and went in, depositing Les on the bed, which was covered with a powder-blue satin spread.

"Go see if you can find that doctor," Ruff said to Staggs. The big man nodded, looked once at Les, and backed out. "And close the door, Harlon."

Les Coyle had been fighting to sit up, so Ruff let him try. The marshal gave a groan and quickly sagged back down.

"Happy now?" Ruff asked.

"Head hurts . . ."

"It should," Justice said, looking at the marshal's scalp. He needed some stitching up, and there was a lump the size of an egg. "Who did it, Les?"

Coyle looked around as if to make sure no one else was in the room. "A man named Campbell. Sal Campbell. He works for Chase Longden."

"You sure?"

"Reasonably. He had on a hood, but Campbell wears silver spurs. When he kicked me in the head, I had a chance to spot them," Les said dryly.

"All right, lie back."

Coyle obeyed, holding his forehead. "Sorry to ruin your homecoming."

"Hell with that. Just take it easy."

"Sure. I got a nice easy job. I rest a lot. Hell, Ruff, I'm used to this. That's why I think sometimes . . . What am I getting Lily into?"

"Let her worry about that. Did this Campbell get away?" Justice asked.

"Afraid so. This toy sword wasn't much of a weapon."

"Chase is getting impatient, then."

"I guess. He knows I won't let up on him, and—"

The doctor entered the room, the light behind him glaringly bright. It was the strangest doctor Ruff had seen in a long time. He was dressed in buckskins and a coonskin cap, wearing a mask, and carrying a muzzle loader and a little black bag. He gave the ancient weapon to Ruff.

"Here, hold this," the doctor said gruffly. "Damn all, Les, you got to ruin everything, don't you? There I was, wrapped up nicely with my wife, who I damn seldom get to see, and a glass of the Duchess's rum. And what happens? The same thing that happened on my wedding and anniversary: the marshal gets himself banged up."

The doctor was garrulous, but he worked as he talked, examining the skull wound, feeling for fractures, running his hands over Les Coyle's ribs. Les winced, and the doctor nodded.

"Just as I figured. Damn, Les, what are you trying to do, hiding something like that?" He looked at Ruff Justice. "The marshal got those busted ribs last week. Three bums from Blue Boy Weaver's place tried to break the marshal up in an alley. He shot two of them, one of them fatally. The other got away. I wanted to check him over that night. You ever have broken ribs? You know how a man moves real carefully and breathes slowly so as not to aggravate anything? Well, I knew Les had them. He thinks he has to go on for the town's sake. Think Denver cares?"

Ruff said he didn't imagine so. Les grinned, and the doctor ignored him, prattling on about his last wedding anniversary when Coyle had gotten himself stabbed, stitching the scalp wound as he talked.

Finished at last, the doctor said, "Now you stay in bed, Les. You promise me."

"I promise."

"Good. See that you do."

The doctor picked up his muzzle loader, adjusted his mask, and headed out. "I'll see you in the morning," he said.

"All right. Thanks, Doc."

After the door had closed, Les Coyle sat up, wincing. He swung his legs over the side of the bed and shook his head while taking in a deep breath.

"What are you doing?" Ruff asked the blond man.

"What the hell do you think I'm doing? I'm getting up, Ruff."

"You heard the doctor. You don't have to go after Campbell now. You've got deputies."

"Who said anything about Campbell? Ruff, in a little while they're going to announce our engagement downstairs. I won't let Lily stand up alone. I mean to be a part of the engagement, the marriage, and all that."

The marshal started to rise, then sagged onto the bed with a moan. His face was still scabbed, his hair matted with blood, his costume ripped to shreds.

"You look like you're going to go down and stand up with Lily," Justice teased. "Why don't you take the doctor's advice?"

"Sure, like you would, Ruffin?" Les Coyle laughed. "Help me up and help me get washed. Then you can strip off that costume and let me wear it."

"You're crazy, Les."

"Sure, we all are. It's a crazy world. Come on, Justice. I don't have that much time. Let me borrow your costume."

Justice shook his head. He had doubts about this, but it was Les' business. Beneath his pirate pants he wore black trousers, and beneath his pirate shirt he had on nothing at all, so he would have to sit in the room and wait for Les to return. Unless Staggs could shake up a shirt somewhere. Maybe some of the Duke's clothes were still in some closet.

The Duchess came in as Les Coyle was adjusting the eye patch. "Ruff?" Then she blinked and turned toward Justice, who was sitting in a chair, shirtless, hands clasped behind his head. "You call yourself a friend?" Katie Price said in astonishment. "Les, I just talked to Doctor Hodges, and he told me you were supposed to be on your back in that bed."

"I recover fast," Coyle said, turning. The bandanna on his head covered the scalp wound, so he didn't look half-bad, except for the minor swelling on his cheekbone.

"And you'll die just as fast. Are you crazy? Both of you?" She looked from Coyle to Ruff, who could only shrug.

"He doesn't want to miss the engagement announcement," Justice said.

"Miss it? He'll miss the wedding. He'll be having a funeral instead." She patted her dark, piled hair into place. "Well, I know I'm wasting my time talking to men like you. Hardheaded. No wonder that knock on the head didn't kill you, Marshal. I wonder if it even hurt. All right, I'll tell Lily you're all right. I'm not above an occasional lie. And we'll go ahead as planned." She started out, halted, and turned to Ruff. "Damn all, Justice, get a shirt on, you're just too tempting to look at."

Then she went out, slamming the door, and Coyle laughed. The movement caused his ribs to ache, and he stopped abruptly, holding his side.

"You could have told me you knew the lady, Ruff."

"I *knew* her, yes," Ruff said. "Now I don't know. Was it all on the up and up when she inherited the mine, Les?"

"The lawyers said so."

"And the murder was—"

"They found the Duke in an alley, pockets empty, head bashed in. Anyone could have done it for any reason. Why?" Coyle asked. "Do you know something I don't know, Justice?"

"Not me, Les. I don't know a damn thing. I just want to see you get engaged, and maybe spend some time with the lady that just left; then I want to get north to Dakota, catch up on some sleep, and get back to doing whatever the army has for me."

"Uh-huh," Les Coyle muttered. He knew Justice well, as well as anyone knew this hard man with the romance in his soul; this rough country scout who craved city women, silks and satins, civilized food and manners; this man who would do anything for a friend and cut an enemy down with the blink of an eye. Ruff had his reasons for asking, but what they were Les Coyle didn't know.

"All set?" Justice asked.

"I guess. You coming?"

"I want a shirt first. I don't want to go as nature boy. Find Staggs or the Duchess. See if this Duchamp-Villon left any clothes."

"All right. It'll just be a minute," the blond pirate said. But it was going to be much longer than that. The marshal winked at Ruff Justice, stepped through the doorway to the bedroom, and was cut down by the sudden barrage of bullets.

The gun opened up and lead hacked the door to splinters, tearing into Les Coyle's body and slamming him backward into a rapidly spreading pool of his own blood.

Ruff Justice leapt for the door, snatching his Colt .41 from its holster. Below, the ballroom was in panic—women's screams mingled with men's violent curses and angry shouts. The orchestra ground to a dissonant, crashing halt.

Justice dashed into the hallway and saw the dark figure of a man sprinting away from him. Justice cut loose, but either he missed or the little New Line revolver didn't have the shocking power to take a man down. The unknown assailant ran on until he reached the end of the hall, where an arched, stained-glass window was framed. He crashed through it, hurtling toward the ground below, glass flying in colored shards.

Justice sprinted after him, pausing only a brief second at the window before he too leapt to the ground below. He landed hard, crouched against the earth, eyes searching, hand wrapped around the revolver.

Nothing moved. A horse nickered somewhere. From inside voices hummed, grew louder as they neared Ruff, and then a tumbling crowd flowed out onto the dark lawn, the glare from the open doorway half-blinding

Justice so that he knew he had no chance of spotting movement or tailing the gunman.

He stood, shirtless, chest heaving, hair in his eyes, gun in hand, and walked toward the open door. The Duchess was there and he asked her about Les without speaking. She shook her head.

"He's dead, Ruff."

"Did anyone see the gunman?"

"No. Didn't you?"

"A glimpse, nothing more." He looked to the house, where the orchestra had once again started to play, sounding bitter, out of place. "Has anyone told Lily?"

"The doctor. He's with her."

They stood there helplessly for a long while. Men spread out across the grounds, looking foolish and a little bizarre in their costumes. But the killer was long gone.

"What now, Ruff?" the Duchess asked.

"You know what. We find him," Ruff said soberly.

"How?"

"I don't know how; I don't care how. When I find him, he's going to die, and I don't care how he does that either."

"It won't help Les any."

"It didn't help him any to be shot full of holes. Sorry, girl, I believe in vengeance, hard vengeance. It doesn't help the dead, but it just might help the next good man who is slated to die. There will be vengeance."

"I had hoped . . ." The Duchess let her voice trail off.

"Yes, so had I. It was a night for it, but they've colored it crimson. They came and took a life, and neither one of us could make love tonight, could we?"

She didn't answer. She squeezed Ruff's arm and went off to see how Lily was doing.

Ruff Justice, knowing there wasn't much hope of finding anything, moved into the darkness to hunt for a killer, thinking black and bloody thoughts of vengeance.

It was useless, as Justice had feared. They combed the grounds, several of the citizens with a little too much liquor under their belts, scaring the wits out of one another. A shot was fired in panic and everyone rushed toward the sound, but it was only a nervous finger on a too-light trigger. In the end, they had nothing to show for their time.

Still shirtless, Ruff went back to the house to find the Duchess looking sober and sedate. She was white in contrast to the shadows surrounding her as she waited in the doorway of the big house. Behind her there was still bright color, bunting, and the brassy glare of band instruments, but there no longer was any cheer to it.

"Nothing?" she asked. There wasn't much hope in the question.

Ruff Justice shook his head. "No, he took off. We'll find him, though."

"Will we?"

Ruff's answer was grim. "Yes, Duchess, we will. I will—I promise you."

"Come on in and get warm, Ruff. Where's your shirt anyway?"

"I'm afraid Les was wearing it." Justice slipped his pistol into his little shoulder holster. "How's Lily holding up?"

"How do you think? It's bad enough when the man you love gets killed, but when it happens on the night you're going to officially announce your engagement . . . it's not easy. Doc is with her, but what can he do except give her a few stiff belts? Which, knowing Doc, he's already done, and taken a few himself."

"She's related to you, isn't she?" Ruff asked as they

crossed the ballroom. A few ladies stood in a cluster, watching them go.

"Her mother was my mother's cousin," Lily said. "I'm not sure what that makes us. I'm not good at that sort of thing, and it's not that important, anyway. I like her. She's my friend, not a relative."

Staggs was coming toward them as they reached the far side of the room. He carried a white linen shirt with French cuffs. In his hand was a pair of onyx cuff links. He gave them to Ruff as Katie Price and Justice entered the library beyond the ballroom.

Ruff slipped into the shirt and fastened the cuff links as Katie poured herself a stiff brandy. She turned, leaning against a reading desk where a leather-bound volume of Dickens lay open.

"What do you keep Staggs around for?" Ruff asked.

"He needs someplace. Everybody needs someplace."

"He doesn't have a very savory background."

"I know that far better than you, Ruff, far better," the former saloon owner said. "But I like to have someone with a little bulk around just in case. Maybe I've gotten a little nervous since the Duke was killed."

Ruff didn't answer. There was a tap at the sliding doors behind them and a thin, nervous man with hound's eyes, hat in hand, entered, his neck bowed as if he were afraid of thumping his head on the ceiling, which he was nearly tall enough to do. There was a star on his faded blue shirt.

"Miss . . . Duchess," he said.

"Hello, Jody. Ruff, this is Jody Sharpe. He's the number-one deputy marshal. I guess acting marshal now."

The two men shook hands. Jody Sharpe's grip was dry, scaly, nearly limp. "I heard of you," Jody said. "Hear the marshal's dead. What happened?"

They told him, and Jody Sharpe bowed his head and looked at them as if he were a shy child. He was deferential and seemingly backward, but Ruff knew Les Coyle, and he hadn't hired any incompetents to back him up. Now and then a quick flash of intelligence would spark in Jody's eyes, and Ruff knew the man was a lot sharper than he let on.

When they had finished telling Jody what had happened, he looked up and said, "Uh-huh. I'll get Campbell, all right. But would you mind telling me who the hell they were trying to kill?"

"I don't understand you," the Duchess said. She seemed irritated, but she was probably just tired.

"I think I do," Ruff said.

"Will one of you explain it to me, then? Please."

"Just this, miss . . . Duchess," Jody said, wringing the hat he held. "The marshal, from what you've told me, was wearing a costume. But it wasn't the costume he came to the party in."

"No, it was Ruff's . . . Oh!"

"Exactly," the deputy said. "He was wearing a pirate costume. He had a bandanna over his blond hair, an eye patch on, and it was a sudden thing. A man would guess he was shooting someone else, unless he knew they had switched costumes."

"But why?" she asked, her voice filled with worry.

"I couldn't guess," Jody replied. "All I know is that a man would have to be awful quick at recognizing the marshal, the way things were described to me. Too quick. No, miss, the way I see it, there's only one possibility. The man who killed Les Coyle was after this man. He wanted to kill Ruff Justice."

The Duchess looked at Justice. "Ruff?"

"He may be right."

"You just arrived in Denver!"

"Yes, but I left a few enemies behind the last time through. Like Angel Farmer."

"Ugh," the Duchess said, recalling the greasy, pocked man.

"Yeah. Unless he's caught a bullet and saved someone some rope?"

Jody shook his head. "He's alive and breathing. What did you run into him over?"

"He and I have different ideas on how you treat a lady," Ruff said.

"Angel Farmer tried to rape one of my girls," Kate Price said. "Justice stopped it fast. With a bullet."

"The only problem was that I put that round in the wrong place. Should have put it in his black little heart."

"Hard man, aren't you?" Jody commented.

"That's right," Justice said. "When are we going?"

"Where?" the deputy asked, putting his hat on.

"I figured you had some work to do this night."

"Yes, I do. I'm going to stop by the office and pick up a scatter-gun. Then I'm going to go down to Chase Longden's place and find Sal Campbell. Maybe he didn't kill the marshal, but he was in a brawl with him, and he's the best suspect we've got."

"I'm going along."

"I don't see a star on you, Mister Justice."

"I don't need one for what I've got in mind. In fact, it might just get in the way."

"Hard man," the deputy repeated. He pondered the idea and shook his head. "I guess I can't keep you away. Come along, where I can keep an eye on you." He started to turn and then added, "Justice, Les was more than a boss. He was my friend, too. We'll get him, no matter who it was. We'll get him."

Justice didn't have any doubts at all about that. Les

Coyle was a good man; he was a tough lawman with a heart; he was a friend. Now he was dead. Yes, they were going to get whoever it was, and when they did, maybe they would have the opportunity to save the town a little more rope.

4

Justice was in buckskins, wearing a white stetson with a red scarf for a band. He had a big blue Colt revolver strapped on. At the back of his belt hung a razor-edged bowie knife. He left his thunder gun, his .56-caliber Spencer repeater, which pushed those five-hundred-grain bullets through its black bore, figuring he wasn't going to meet a man big enough to take that much killing.

Jody had been watching Justice dress, amazed at the size the man seemed to take on as he slipped into his range clothes, at the way the fine long hair, hanging past the man's shoulders, seemed less an affectation and more a badge of male pride. He had worn that mane in Sioux territory, in Comanche country, and he still had his scalp. The hands Justice used to strap up were large and hardened; the eyes were deep blue, as if the sky had been captured there, the big sky, the wild-country sky. He was a hard man, and Jody knew he was seeing something special. The stories came back, the tales the marshal liked to tell of Justice and the Windwolf and the long winter wars, the Spirit Woman and the Denver shoot-outs.

There was time for all these thoughts to go through Jody's mind, but Justice was hardly dallying. He was dressed, armed, and ready to start out in a few minutes.

"I might have gotten lead into Campbell, or whoever it was," Ruff said.

"You did. I found blood in the corridor, a few spots on the grass below the window. Couldn't follow it far, though."

Ruff nodded with respect. The deputy knew his work, and had done it well. "Damned little New Line didn't have the thump to put the man down."

"That one does," Jody said, nodding at the long-barreled .44 pistol at Ruff's waist.

"Yes," Justice agreed. "This one does."

"Shall we give it a chance?"

"Yes, Deputy, let's do just that."

Jody could have picked up a couple more deputies, but they had their own duties, and if the two of them couldn't handle Campbell, the marshal figured they might as well both leave the territory.

Besides, they were in a hurry. They wanted Campbell, and they wanted him now. They wanted to find the man and see if he had a fresh gunshot wound. They wanted to close the investigation quickly, preferably with Campbell trying to fight back.

Delaney Street hadn't improved any since Ruff Justice last saw it. Sleazy saloons, cheap cribs rife with disease, at least two Chinese opium dens, homes for the lost and crippled, a ramshackle store dealing mostly in liquor and cartridges, cheap knives, and flashy silks.

Chase Longden's place was a castle among the smaller places of iniquity and perversion. Two-storied, blazing with light, alive with sound and motion, it dominated the street, challenged only by the opposing hell hole, which was owned by Chase's former partner, the massive and formidable Blue Boy Weaver.

Both men had made their fortunes by blackmailing prominent citizens who had frequented their places, by threatening established merchants, by knocking miners on the head in dark alleys to relieve them of their pokes, through prostitution and the opium trade. They were a lovely pair.

"How you want to do this?" Jody asked, deferring for reasons of his own to Ruff's judgment.

"If you wouldn't mind going around back with that scatter-gun, I'll go in the front door. I don't know Campbell, but if he's the one that took lead, I'll find him. Just keep me out of the line of fire if you have to cut that buckshot loose."

"Justice, Longden won't like this. He doesn't tolerate the law much. He tried to kill Les once, you know, during his trial. He won't take to a civilian barging in there wanting blood."

"Thanks for the warning," Justice said, but it was obvious from his tone that he wasn't going to be deterred.

"I'll go in the back . . . If you see Longden, watch for a sleeve gun. He's good with it."

It told Ruff something about the kind of man he was dealing with, knowing that Chase Longden wore a sleeve gun. They were quick, deadly, sneaky as a rattler in shed. It was a killing weapon, not one to do battle with, but one to eliminate your opponent with before the battle could begin. It was a murderer's weapon.

Ruff waited in the shadows until he figured Jody had had enough time to reach the back door of Longden's saloon. He watched a few drunk miners stagger past, a cowboy mounted backward on his horse ride down the center of Delaney Street, a Chinese woman of twenty or so stand in the alley beside the opium palace showing her knee to a passing man who took her up on the offer.

Ruff checked the fit of his Colt in his holster and went through the green-painted door into the bright, raucous, obnoxious interior of Chase Longden's place.

The bar was two deep with miners, their boots and pants muddy, their hands raw and red, their faces bearded, hard, affable. Two girls in silk skirts and petticoats were doing some kind of a dance on a platform at the far end of the long room. A piano seemed to be playing an accompaniment, but it was hard to be sure above the constant clink and chatter and roar and whine of the saloon.

Ruff moved inside easily, but he was noticed immediately by two redheaded men, probably brothers, wearing dark suits and diamond rings. They had huge sideburns and unhappy pale eyes. And right then, they seemed to be unhappy with Ruff Justice.

They moved his way. Justice watched them and glanced simultaneously at the floor, where a few crimson spots were slowly soaking into the wood.

"Want something?" the bigger of the redheaded men asked out of the side of his mouth as they eased up beside Ruff.

"How about Chase Longden?"

"Chase don't know you."

"How do you know?"

The man shook his head. "He don't know you."

"All right. Where's Sal Campbell?"

"Who?" The man looked appropriately blank. He was enjoying himself. "Hear of such a man, Ed?" he asked his partner. That one might have been dumb—he just grinned and shook his head. "Nope, we don't know him. Why don't you just ease on out? Unless there was something else?"

"One more thing." Ruff toed the floor. "How about showing me the man who left this here?"

"That blood? That was the butcher bringing a load of beefsteaks in."

"This time of night?"

"Yeah. I said so, didn't I? What are you trying to do, tall man, make me out a liar?"

"You're making yourself out to be one," Justice said, and the redhead tensed. Justice, he realized suddenly, wasn't going to be bluffed. He was going to have to be taught a lesson.

"Chase Longden don't like your type hanging around. So scoot!"

"Sure—when Longden tells me," Justice answered. "Where is he?"

"I said, scoot," the redhead hissed, and stepped in, reaching for his gun. It was so quick that no one saw when Justice made his move. He drew his .44 and shot the big man through the thigh, and he went down with a howl of pain as the shot racketed through the saloon. The other man tried to pull a knife, but Justice slashed him across the face with the still-smoking barrel of his Colt, and he too went down in a heap, the knife clattering free as the clamor inside the bar gave way to a concerted cry of alarm, and the crowd parted.

Across the length of the saloon, Justice saw Jody standing with his shotgun, both hammers cocked. It was enough to clear any room anytime.

"You all right, Justice?"

"Just fine." Ruff glanced at the men at his feet, the one writhing, holding an injured leg, the other still out cold. "Can you tell me where we can find Longden now?"

"Right here," the man to Ruff's right said, and Justice looked that way to see the gambler and saloon operator Chase Longden. He was shorter than Ruff had expected, more rounded. His hair was black and sleek, his eyes hooded. "Who are you and what the hell do you want?"

"Conversation."

"Hell of a way to go about it. Charley? Go find Doc or the barber. Get these two sewed up and then give them their pay. They can't do the job, I don't want them."

They dragged the redheaded men away, and Longden watched without expression.

"Let's talk," Jody said, approaching Longden with the shotgun still at the ready.

"You gone crazy, Jody? Does Les know you're out here playing with guns?"

"Les Coyle is dead," Jody said.

"That's tough."

"We want to talk to you about it."

"Me? I been here all night. Ask anyone."

"Let's talk," Jody repeated, and there was a toughness in his voice now.

Longden shrugged. "All right. Come into my office. You're costing me money."

He turned and led the way, and the piano player started up again. But it didn't do much to liven things up. The miners watched silently, hardly moving, until Ruff and Jody had entered Longden's office and closed the door behind them. Then Ruff heard the excited murmuring.

Longden entered his office imperiously, sat at a huge green-leather-covered desk, and lit a cigar, folding his hands together to peer over them with his dark, hooded eyes.

"What's all this about, Jody?"

"The marshal's dead."

"So you said. Am I supposed to cry? Who's that with you? Wait a minute! Ruff Justice."

"That's it. Now that the introductions are over," Ruff said, "where's Sal Campbell?"

"Who?"

"Sal Campbell," Jody said. "He still works for you, doesn't he, Longden?"

"No, you got that wrong. He never worked for me. He just kind of hung around picking up a little change now and then for odd jobs."

"Like killing Marshal Coyle?"

"Sal? He never had that kind of nerve."

"He had enough nerve to jump Coyle tonight and try to beat him up."

"Who said?"

"Coyle."

"Oh, well, he won't be saying it anymore, will he?"

Jody started forward, but Ruff held him back. The deputy was rigid with anger now. Justice could feel it in his muscles and tendons. Ruff wasn't any happier, but he was controlling his rage a little better.

"Where's Campbell?" Ruff asked quietly.

"I said I didn't know, Justice."

"Did that butcher bring those steaks in your office, too?"

"Huh?" Longden blinked. "What the hell are you talking about?"

"There are spots of blood on your floor."

"The hell!" But Longden rose and looked around, his face telling Ruff plainly that there *could* have been blood there. Longden froze, his smile crooked around the cigar in his teeth. "Wise guy. Now I remember something about you, Justice. You were always a wise bastard."

"Sure. Where's Campbell?"

"No idea." Longden sagged back into his chair, looking pleased with himself.

"All right," Jody said, "we're going to search your place."

"Now wait a minute . . ."

"You wait. We're going to search it, and if there's any more trouble from you or any of your thugs, I'm going to look at it as interfering with an officer of the law during the performance of his duty. That means jail."

"It means bail and big trouble for you. Judge Ellis—"

"Don't threaten me, Longden. It means jail, and a night in our jail right now could be pretty uncomfortable if you understand me."

"Sure, Jody, I understand," he said, but then the man cocked his arm in an odd way, and Justice saw the pistol slip into his palm from the sleeve mechanism. Justice stepped in and cracked the saloonkeeper's wrist with his pistol. The gun fell free as bone broke and Longden screamed with pain.

"Damn you, damn you, Justice, you're a dead man for that!"

"We're going to search your place now," Jody said. "You do understand now, Chase?"

"Yeah," he panted through the pain, "I understand now." His eyes were dark with killing fire.

Chase wouldn't forget this. Justice half-hoped he wouldn't. He hadn't been instantly charmed by the man.

Outside, two of Longden's boys were cleaning up. Jody said, "If you found the doctor, tell him Chase Longden needs a little work too."

Hostile eyes followed them as they crossed the saloon and went to the stairway in the back of the room. They started up, Ruff pausing to point at the carpeting. There was one small spot of blood there, and it was very recent.

They went about it the only way they could. Room by room.

The first was empty and cold. The second was alive with heat.

It smelled of sweat and of human effort. There were two people in the room, both energetic. The one on top was a round, white male, the one on the bottom was female and a lot darker.

Both of them were fleet of foot.

As the door opened, the man rolled aside, his eyes wide, and he made for the window as the Oriental woman snatched the blanket around her bulbous breasts, cursing in a lost language. Ruff smiled, walked to the closet, opened it, looked under the bed on the off chance, and started out.

"Reverend Slade," Jody muttered. "I can hardly believe it."

"He's a man too."

"Yeah, but the way he rails . . . I believe I'll change churches."

The next room down the corridor was also occupied, but the man inside wasn't so spry. He was dead, lying on a rumpled bed, which was soaked in blood.

Jody looked at the man. "Sal Campbell," he told Ruff. "Looks like it was him that killed the marshal. Looks like you got him."

Ruff nodded. "Maybe." He looked at the silver spurs on the black boots, at the gray, formless face.

"Maybe?" Jody had eased down the hammers on his ten-gauge shotgun. "What do you mean?"

"Why didn't he kill Coyle when he had a chance the first time?"

"Why? Hell, I don't know. Maybe he had to go home and get a gun. Maybe he wasn't mad until Coyle fought back."

"Maybe it wasn't Campbell that came back. Maybe Campbell beat up the marshal, ran off, and came back here. Then someone else killed Coyle. Thinking it was me, maybe, I don't know about that."

"What happened to Campbell, Justice? There's a hole in his back that you put there while he was running away from you."

"Did I put it there?" Ruff asked.

"Who else?"

"I don't know, Deputy, unless it was someone who wanted to place the blame for the murder on Campbell. Hell, we'd believe that easily enough. Sure, Coyle told us it was Campbell. So why not believe Campbell was the murderer? That would take the heat off quick enough—except Campbell would protest. So kill him."

"You have some unusual ideas, Justice."

"Yes. I also carry an unusual sidearm when I'm in town."

"I don't get you."

"How many men do you know that carry a forty-one pistol? It's a woman's caliber. I carry the New Line because it fits under a town suit. I can't tote this Peacemaker around everywhere I go."

"So?"

"So, let's have that bullet taken out of Campbell's back. What do you want to bet it's not a forty-one?"

"You're serious, aren't you?"

"Damn right. I have a feeling, Jody, like the feeling you had that whoever killed Les meant to gun me down. I didn't shoot Sal Campbell. I didn't kill him because he wasn't even there. He's just the patsy. His pals killed him to lay off the blame."

"Maybe . . ." Jody said reluctantly.

"Dig out the bullet. Let's see. I'll give you odds it's a forty-four or a thirty-six caliber. I haven't seen a man in months carrying a forty-one. Have a look, Jody—and a little advice, don't leave the body."

"I won't. Where are you going?"

"To find the doctor and send him up, unless you want to carve that lead out yourself. Then," Justice said, "I'm going back to the Duchess's house. There's a little more investigating to be done there."

He winked and Jody frowned, not getting it, but then he didn't know the sort of investigation Ruff Justice had in mind.

He didn't know because he was tired and the night outside was cold. And because he didn't know that sometime, somewhere a hundred years ago Ruff had slept close to Katie Price long before she had been the Duchess of Denver, and tasted the sweet femininity of her, the tender skilled flesh of the woman working against his.

It had been too long.

She was awake, the Duchess of Denver, sitting in an overstuffed white chair in her drawing room, wearing a white dressing gown of silky material that dropped to the floor but parted at the knee to give Justice a tantalizing preview. There was white fur on the hem, at the cuffs, and around the neck like a framing softness that somehow both blurred and focused the classic dark head of Katie Price. She looked just a little weary now, perhaps a little drunk. She still had that brandy snifter in her hand.

"Well, you came back alive," she said.

"You can't have all the luck."

"Not funny. Not tonight, Justice."

"No." He sat on the arm of her chair and rubbed her sleek neck with his hand. Her head lolled back contentedly. "It's not so funny tonight."

"Did you have any luck? Did you find him?"

Ruff told her about Campbell. "But I'll bet whatever you like that they don't find my bullet in him. Someone took the thug and killed him to frame him."

"Chase Longden?"

"If so, it was pretty stupid of Longden to do the job in his own place. I doubt Longden is that stupid."

Ruff's interest was drifting. He slid his free hand down inside the silky top of the dressing gown, letting it run over the smooth warm flesh of Katie Price's breast, finding the taut, eager nipple. She looked up at him with starry eyes and kissed his hand.

"It's late," she said in a blurred voice.

"Very late," Justice said, and he bent to kiss her, tasting the sweetness of her lips, the lingering flavor of brandy there, his head filling with the faint perfume. She had bathed while he was out—bathed and then waited up.

"Let's go to bed," she suggested sensibly.

She handed Ruff the snifter, which he placed aside on the ebony table. Then the Duchess of Denver rose, a little unsteadily, Ruff thought.

"Sure you're up to this?" he asked with a grin.

"Sure you are?"

"What do you think, Katie?" He pulled her to him and kissed her again, the weight of her body familiar, the touch of her lips enticing. She rested her cheek on his chest.

"So long, it's been so long. Damn you, Ruff Justice. Why can't you be a settling-down man? Why did you have to go? We had a good thing."

"Yes," Justice said quietly. "We had a good thing."

"And I want a little of it now." She looked up into his eyes and he smiled.

"All right. I'm not all that genteel just now." He laughed. His trousers were smudged, his face dirty, his hands torn, his hair wild.

"I'll wait. Take a bath."

"How? I don't want to wake anyone to boil water and carry it."

"Where have you been?" the Duchess asked. "I've got a copper boiler in my basement with thirty gallons of hot water in it right now. I know—I stoked the coal box myself while you were gone."

"Oh! And how does it get to my room, or do I go to the basement?"

"No, you wait in the marble bathtub upstairs for the water to come through the copper pipe that runs up there—and most of the time it comes."

Ruff was willing to believe it. After all, they did have running water at the Grand Hotel, but in a private home? The Duchess's manor, however, was hardly typical. She had marble statuary hidden in small alcoves here and there, gold and silver objects strewn around like debris scattered by the wind. Everything glittered and gleamed. There were deep-red, velvet curtains and white carpets, jade ornaments, and an indoor black marble fountain and pond.

And, yes, the fittings in the bathroom were plated with gold. "See what you've been missing?" the Duchess asked, her moving hand indicating the bathroom, which was mirrored, polished, and high-ceilinged. The copper bathtub sat in the center of the room.

"Show me," Ruff Justice said, and the Duchess, far from coy, did.

She stepped from her dressing gown like a moth shedding its silky cocoon. And there she stood, Katie Price, with a pearl necklace around her throat; with breasts full and firm, uptilted, nipples ripe and tender. The sleek length of her thighs ended at the luxurious dark patch between them. She was lean and familiar and eager.

"Well?" she asked.

"You've shown me." And Ruff showed her, as well. He stepped from his buckskins and waited before her, hard and capable, his lips forming a tight, suppressed smile.

She came to him, one hand reaching around to mold itself to his buttock, the other cradling his manhood. Her lips were parted, and she breathed softly and raggedly as she gripped him and pulled him near her soft bush, her head thrown back, her long dark hair beginning to fall free of the elaborate pinning.

"Well?" she repeated.

Justice just held her, her warm naked body next to his. He remembered. They had spent that winter together beneath quilts and comforters most of the time, laughing and making love, clinging to each other as if it were to be the last winter. But it wasn't—other winters had come and gone and forgetfulness had taken control.

"Turn the tap," she said, stepping back, flushed not only in the face, but down across her breasts.

"Hot water's going to come out there, is it?" Ruff said, turning away. He bent slightly to turn the tap, feeling Katie's finger run up along the line between his hard buttocks, feeling her step in closer, wrap her arms around him, and press her breasts to his back as the water began to flow, cool at first and then gradually hotter until steam filled the bathroom, fogging the mirrors. Ruff turned, picked Katie up high and, unable to wait any longer, let her wrap those magnificent thighs around his waist, let her reach for his rising erection and slip it effortlessly into her soft warmth.

"I've needed you for a long time," she said into his ear, her breath as warm and steamy as the room, her body slick with moisture, her dark hair all a-tumble as she reached behind her, found Ruff's sack, and pressed it against her.

"Oh, God!" she breathed. Her head was back, her eyes distant, her body a swaying thing, alive, strong, and desperate as she reached a quick hard climax.

"The bath," Ruff said after a long while.

She unwrapped her legs and stood shaking against him. Justice turned off the tap and then slid from her, still hard, still ready. Katie watched him, the movements of his body, the fascinating maleness of him, wanting to reach for him, to devour him, to submit to him.

Justice stepped into the huge copper tub and she followed. He slid into the water and leaned back. The Duchess sat facing him, easing herself down, her legs on top of his. She was smiling wickedly and Justice laughed out loud, leaning forward to wrap his hand in her hair and draw her to him.

The Duchess lifted her legs and slung them over the sides of the tub, and Justice let his hands run along her inner thighs, let his thumbs part her. He bent his head to kiss her, and she shuddered, her hands caressing his hair.

The water was warm, the room quiet and away from everything black and bloody and noisy. Ruff leaned back again, his head on the rim of the tub. Katie began to wash him with a bar of lilac-scented soap. She worked up his legs and across his stomach, her fingers diligent, searching, knowing, and when she was finished, she asked, "To bed?"

"If you want." Ruff opened one lazy eye. She was watching him eagerly, this naked beautiful thing, this woman who was all woman, yet tough enough and wise enough—perhaps even courageous enough—to have survived on Delaney Street; who had married the Duke and risen above Denver's scorn; who now gave the impression, true or not, that there had been only one purpose to her life: the loving of Ruff Justice.

She dried him with a thick towel, carefully rubbing his thighs, the heavy maleness of him, stroking, petting, and kissing him until they made a virtual dash for the bed. The Duchess rolled over onto her belly and spread her legs, groping for Ruff, not satisfied until she had tugged him into her, until her body had become a writhing, single-minded thing that wanted only completion, which she soon found. She opened her mouth in a soundless scream, and Ruff Justice slid it in to the hilt and found his own draining climax.

Then the Duchess rolled onto her back without losing him, and her arms went around his neck. She kissed him and pulled him down, holding him as if her life would end if she let him go, and the night spun away, warm and satiny and delicious.

Only once that night did Ruff awake from his heavy, sated sleep. He listened to the night, his heart thumping, his body next to the curved and comforting body of Katie Price, smelling her, feeling her clasping him even as she slept.

Nothing moved in the dark house, but something had awakened him—and then he recalled the dream, the star of blood, the moaning creatures surrounding him, the pirate with the skull for a face, the pain and thunder and flame. He drew closer yet to Katie, touching her until she awakened and sleepily reached for him, giving comfort to his need.

5

They had breakfast in bed. A short, thin Chinese girl without expression came into their bedroom and served them on trays. Katie had been up, obviously. Someone had ordered the food, and she was wearing a blue dressing gown, her hair scented and combed, her face already made up.

Ruff sat up shaking his head, bare-chested, woozy, feeling exhausted but fine, very fine indeed. Then Katie was next to him in bed again, propped up on three fat pillows. As the Chinese girl went away, closing the door softly behind her, Katie leaned over to him and tasted his lips with her tongue.

"Eat," she said. "It's no good cold."

Katie Price knew how to eat well. Maybe the Duke had taught her some of it. Smoked ham and fresh trout, lime-orange marmalade on muffins, eggs with soft white cheese melted over them, and mushrooms and capers folded in. They had Turkish coffee and orange slices for dessert, though where they'd come from Ruff couldn't have guessed.

"This is damned near obscene," Justice said.

"Maybe. I have to do something with the money. I'll show you my fifty-thousand-dollar fox cape, and you tell me what's obscene."

"It comes from seeing hungry people," Ruff said.

"Indians."

"Some of 'em."

"They have all the best furs," Katie said, and Ruff half-smiled.

"How much money have you got, Katie?"

"People don't usually ask questions like that."

"I thought we knew each other well enough."

"Maybe." She squeezed his arm and snuggled against him. "Are you serious? You want to know?"

"Sure."

"Well, maybe it'll make you want to stay with me. They tell me it's something like twenty million."

"I wasn't joking, Katie."

"Neither was I, Ruff Justice."

He nodded and finished the last bite of a biscuit and then drank his coffee. "So folks wondered about you and the Duke?"

"What do you mean?" She got it then and sat up, rigid. "You mean did they think I might have killed him for his money? Why, damn you, Ruff . . . Yes, I guess they did at that, except I had a solid alibi."

"All right. I just wanted to know."

"The hell you did. I know you. What's on your mind, Ruffin?" the Duchess asked.

"I've just been worrying this thing over."

"What thing?" she asked. "My marriage, living with me?" she teased.

"Les Coyle."

"Oh." The fun went out of Katie Price's voice. "What's that got to do with me?"

"It happened here."

"Sure!" She wasn't all that amused. "And when I saw that he was on to me for killing the Duke, I shot him. Maybe I just thought he was you in that pirate costume, like Jody said."

"Maybe so."

They were silent for a time; it wasn't that cheerful a conversation, but something was nagging at Ruff, some notion—based not on reason, but on intuition—that the murder of Les Coyle and the Duchess of Denver's life were somehow related.

"I want to know why," Justice said.

Katie softened again; she turned toward him, her bare thigh going over Ruff's.

"Why was Les Coyle murdered? Why was he murdered here and last night?"

"He was killed because he has a lot of enemies, Ruff," Katie said.

"Yes, I know it."

"There's Longden and Blue Boy Weaver; hell, half the saloon people on Delaney Street."

"But why do it last night, Katie?" Ruff asked. "It couldn't have been the most convenient place in the world, nor the most convenient time. Why not get Les when he walks his rounds, or in some dark alley? Why kill him at all? Apparently Longden and these other bums on Delaney Street get some kind of protection from the local judges, this Judge Ellis, for instance."

"How'd you learn about him?"

"I live fast."

"Yes, Ellis is soft on Longden. He has virtual carte blanche."

"Why kill the marshal, then? That's the sort of thing a judge can't protect you over."

"I couldn't say," Katie said.

Ruff kissed her again, his hand reaching for the soft warmth between her legs, and finding it. She kissed him back, but she suddenly seemed distant. He began to wonder if she did know something else. Or maybe the conversation just wasn't conducive to romance.

"I'm going to find out," Ruff said. "I'm going to find out what Les was up to. There has to be a reason. It was a big risk for someone to enter this house and kill him."

"Or try to kill you," Katie pointed out.

"I haven't forgotten that possibility, either. But there can't have been more than a handful of people who knew I was in Denver."

"Like me?"

"Maybe. How did you know, anyway, or did you just happen to come by the marshal's office?"

"Justice, your mind works in mysterious ways. You suspect a woman who's spent the better part of the night making love to you, who feeds you and holds your hand and wants to give you her very milk?"

"You haven't any milk."

"Answer," she said, tasting his lips again, but he changed the subject.

"How's Lily taking it all?"

"Very badly, Ruff. I was down to her room before you woke up, and she hadn't been to sleep all night. She'd been crying. God, her bed was soggy with the tears, her eyes were pitiful."

"You can take care of her, can't you?"

"She doesn't want to be here, Ruffin. She wants to go home."

"Home?"

"To the little house in Colson Canyon, the house she was fixing up for Les."

"Are you going to let her go? Alone?" Ruff swung his

bare feet to the floor and rose, Katie's hand trailing down his back and then falling away.

"If that's the way she wants it. What else can I do?"

"I don't know," he answered, and he didn't. But it always seemed as if there ought to be something people could do at a time like this, something to take away the hurt, like telling them that the dead would be back, that it was a nightmare, a bad dream, a joke of chance. All you could do was watch them cry.

"Where are you going?" Katie asked. Her dressing gown had fallen open and the pink-budded breasts beneath it became visible, summoning and compelling Ruff. He had trouble turning away, dressing in his buckskins.

"Down to the marshal's office. There's a reason Les was killed and I'm going to find it, because once I find the reason, I'll find the killer."

She was silent for a long minute, watching Ruff tug on his pants. "What about the army?" she asked at last. "Don't they want you back?"

"Now you want to chase me away?"

"No, Ruffin. It's just that I don't want you hurt too."

"The hell with that, the hell with the army. They've got along without me for a long while. I have something to do here, something that has to be done. I'm going to find Les's killer, and he's going to pay. He," Ruff said, "or she."

And before Katie Price, looking spoiled and startled and lovely, could answer, Ruff snatched up his shirt and hat and with a wink walked out the door of her fancy bedroom.

Staggs was waiting outside.

Justice stopped, his eyes narrowing. What was Staggs up to? What had he heard?

"Yeah?" Ruff asked the big man.

"Your belongings have been moved to the guest room at the end of the hall, sir," Staggs said, still trying to bring off the cultured tones of a butler in a melodrama, but not quite making it. His nose had been smashed by a mule skinner named Norris, later famed for having killed a grizzly with a bowie knife, though the grizzly had chewed Norris' arm off before he died. Staggs had a cruel mouth, small but with pulpy blue lips. He had one eye narrowed permanently as a result of a cut brow received in a street fight. He wasn't the world's greatest manservant.

"Who asked you to bring my gear over?" Ruff wanted to know.

"The Duchess."

"She did, did she? And you do whatever she asks, do you, Staggs?"

"That's right, Justice," he answered, his voice changing completely, his eyes growing hard. "That lady saved my life once, fed me when I was hungry, gave me a job when no one else would. I do whatever she says. Anything at all."

"Yeah." Ruff nodded, reevaluating things briefly. "All right, Staggs. Show me my room. I might need some of the equipment I've got there."

Like the big .56, which Ruff checked over completely before he stuffed it back into its fringed buckskin sheath. With a nod at the waiting, watching Staggs, Justice went out into the cold, clear daylight of Denver, Colorado.

Ruff didn't have a horse. He supposed the Duchess had some, maybe hundreds or thousands, who knew? But he wanted to walk this morning, to walk down cold and filthy Delaney Street past Blue Boy Weaver's place and Chase Longden's saloon to Grand and from there to the marshal's office. It gave him time to think—not that he came up with anything new or insightful.

The marshal's office was a mess.

Ruff hadn't met the deputy who was trying to clean up the papers that were strewn everywhere, the cold ashes, the overturned desk, the wanted posters ripped from the walls. He had a broom in one hand; his other hand rested on the pearl-handled butt of a Colt revolver.

"Do I know you?" the nearly bald, bug-eyed man asked.

"Likely not. I'm Ruff Justice."

"That's you, is it?" the man asked, but he seemed to relax a little. His hand slid away from the pistol in his holster. "What can I do for you? My name's Ty Roosevelt. Deputy."

"Jody hasn't been in?"

"This is Jody's church morning. He's that kind of a man. He'll be in later."

"What happened here?"

"Got me. Someone wanted something. Broke the door down and maybe took it, maybe didn't."

"Like what?" Ruff asked Ty.

"You go ahead and guess. I couldn't."

The door behind them opened and both men turned toward Jody Sharpe, who wore a dark suit and a doleful expression. " 'Morning, Mister Justice. What's all this, Ty?"

"I don't know. Just got the word an hour ago. Strong door too," he said to himself. "When they wanted to bust Don McGee out of here to lynch him, the mob couldn't crash that oak door down. Not that Les let them have many tries."

Jody crossed the room. "Got into the files, did they?"

"They got into everything."

"Is there any way to tell what's been taken or destroyed?" Ruff Justice asked.

"Not for a time. No."

"Why did they do it, Jody?"

"I really couldn't tell you. Looking for money, maybe," the deputy said.

"In here? Looking for trouble. The person would have to be a maniac to break into the marshal's office to look for money. He would know he'd be lucky if he wasn't killed."

"Then, what?" Jody asked.

"Evidence, I would guess. What was Les working on?"

"Les? He was working on a hundred things, Justice. He really thought he could clean up Denver."

"Don't you, Jody?"

The deputy raised his eyes. "I'm not Les Coyle," he answered.

"I'll tell you one thing," Ty Roosevelt said, "there's not a bit of paper on that Never-Never investigation left in the office."

The name prodded Ruff's interest. "The Duchess's mine? What was Les investigating there?"

"I couldn't tell you right off," Ty said. "All I know is that Burbank and Les were in close conference about something."

"Who is this Burbank?"

"He's the mine manager. Been there since the Duke took over from Willy McDowell and the Ute."

"Then Burbank works for the Duchess."

"Maybe. I guess so. Except he and the Duchess don't seem to see eye to eye on things. Maybe it's because Nathan Burbank has to deal with rock and dust and fire and gas and men, and the Duchess seems to deal mostly in the profits."

"Maybe," Ruff Justice said carefully.

Jody told the other deputy none too discreetly, "Mister Justice is a good friend of the Duchess, and a good friend of Les Coyle. Or he was."

Ty turned his eyes away and didn't say another word while Justice was there. Ruff turned to Jody, who looked like nothing less than a tall, narrow preacher in his dark suit. "Where do I find Nathan Burbank?"

"Why would you want to see him, Justice?"

"I have the feeling I need to."

"I thought you were just interested in finding Les' killer."

"I am. I intend to."

"At the Never-Never?"

"I couldn't say, Jody. Is that where Burbank is, or has he got an office in town?"

"He'll be up there," the deputy said with apparent reluctance. "Seems like a waste of your time, though."

"Maybe. Some folks hold that living is a waste of time—moving around, breathing, eating, and all—when it's obvious that in the end you're just slated for a hole in the ground. What do you think of that, Jody?"

"I couldn't say, Mister Justice."

"No. Oh, Jody, you didn't tell me. That bullet that plugged Campbell. What was it?"

"It was a forty-four, Mister Justice."

"Was it? Good, now I can sleep nights. I'd been worried that I'd killed the gentleman. Now we know I didn't, don't we? That only leaves us with the question of who *did*."

The two deputies didn't seem unhappy to see Justice go.

Ruff hired a horse at a stable, which was sleazy and rickety, but spick-and-span where the horses were kept. A rheumy black man showed him around, hardly speaking, only nodding his head to answer questions.

The horse was a buckskin with a black mane and a colorless, bobbed tail. Why that had been done to it, Ruff didn't know or care. Maybe it had been blowing in some lady's face as she drove her surrey.

But the buckskin didn't seem to have ever been anything but a saddle horse, and a good one at that. Its coat was long with winter fast approaching. It was stubby and deep in the chest, built for long, hard miles, and if they wouldn't be covered in record time, Ruff felt pretty sure he would at least get there.

"Never-Never," Willy McDowell was said to have uttered in despair. Nineteen years in the mountains with hard winters and unpredictable Indians, and he hadn't struck a thing. He was so low he named his mine the Never-Never, and Ruff had heard it said that Willy had started the mine only to have a dugout to spend the winter in.

Then he had struck it big, he and his partner, whom the whites called only "the Ute." Struck it, sold the mine, and drank himself merrily to death all within six months.

Ruff lifted his eyes to the Rockies towering over him, surrounding him with their grandeur. They were all shadow and snow just now. It was already winter in the high country, above the timberline. The deep ranks of pines, which smothered the mountain valleys and the slopes, grew tall and thick.

If it weren't for the wagon road, it would seem that a man had never set foot on this peak . . . the wagon road and the thin finger of smoke rising into the pale-blue sky.

Justice rode with his rifle across the saddlebow, his hat tugged low. It was almost cool enough for him to dig into his roll for a coat. Breath steamed from the nostrils of the ugly buckskin. There was ice along the side of the road here and there where water had settled.

Justice crested a low piny ridge and sat looking at the

Never-Never mine, where men were at work with mules and lumber and stone, while deep inside the earth others carved at the natural vault, risking their lives for meager wages.

Willy McDowell had found it, the Duke had purchased it, Katie Price lived off it.

Ruff started down the wagon road toward the gate below, where two armed men waited, watching silently from beneath their hat brims. They weren't real friendly.

"Get," was all the man on the left said. He was narrow and dark, possibly a half-breed.

"I want to see Mister Burbank," Justice told him.

"We're not hiring."

"I don't want a job," Ruff answered mildly.

"We're not buying."

"I'm not selling."

It was time for the second man to speak up, the man Ruff had recognized immediately and tried to ignore. He was pocked and oily, dangerous-looking. He was a depraved piece of work who got his kicks trying to rape young women. He needed to be killed, but they just hadn't gotten around to it yet, though Justice had tried once a while back.

Angel Farmer was trash and he was mad, killing mad. He knew Justice, all right; he remembered him too well.

"You swing down," Farmer said, his voice hoarse with excitement, with blood lust. "You swing down off that horse, Mister Ruff Justice, because I'm going to kill you right here and right now."

6

"What the hell's the matter with you, Angel?" the swarthy guard asked. He had been ready to bluff and bluster at Justice, to have a little fun turning the man in buckskins around, but Farmer wasn't funning. He was ready to kill. You could see it in his eyes, smell it on him.

"Shut up, Lou."

"You can't shoot a man down—"

"I said, shut up, Lou." Farmer's dark, malevolent eyes returned to Justice. "I said get down, Ruff Justice. Get down and die."

Justice sat his horse a minute longer. The wind drifted his long dark hair, and the horse stamped a hoof and blew impatiently. Lou was backing away very carefully toward the guard shack.

Ruff had his Spencer in his hands, but it was sheathed and it was pointing away from Angel Farmer. By the time he could possibly swing the muzzle around, Farmer would have had time to kill him. Nor could Justice go for his Colt. Farmer had his Winchester aimed at Justice's guts, and he wanted to use it. Oh, did he want to use it.

"Angel . . ." Lou tried murmuring one more time, but Angel Farmer didn't even hear the man.

"Down, Justice. On this side."

Justice got down, but not quite the way Angel Farmer was hoping or expecting. He swung his leg over the buckskin's neck, rifle held high. Kicking his foot out of the stirrup, Ruff threw the Spencer in Angel Farmer's face.

Farmer cursed. The Winchester in his hands exploded with flame and deadly intent. The buckskin danced away in terror. Justice had hit the ground rolling, not away from Farmer, for there wasn't much point in that, but into him. Now he hit Angel's knees, and as Farmer tried desperately to lever another round into the chamber of his Winchester, he was slammed to the ground. Ruff Justice was all over him like a big cat.

Ruff banged a right-hand shot off Farmer's jaw and the man's head thudded back against the earth. He tried to claw at Ruff's eyes, but Justice slapped his hands away and chopped down at Farmer with a left, catching the thug below the ear.

The boots behind Justice warned him, but he couldn't turn in time. Lou had decided to get back into the fight. Now that it didn't appear to be a killing matter but only a chance to beat some stranger senseless, Lou was just another pack dog ready to jump in on downed prey.

He tried to kick Ruff's head off for him, but Justice had had enough warning to allow him to throw himself to one side, though Lou's boot toe nearly ripped Ruff's ear off. Justice came to his feet quickly. Farmer had lifted his Colt from his holster and was coming up two-handed with it. Justice was quicker.

The Colt in Ruff's hand had gotten there before Angel could blink. And now, before Farmer could squeeze off his shot, Ruff's .44 laid a red-hot iron across the badman's thigh. He squealed with pain like a stuck pig, grabbed his leg, and took off into the trees, whining like a bratty kid.

Lou was standing there motionless, hatless, staring at Justice, his own rifle in his hands.

"You want to put that down?" Justice asked quietly. The gun in his hand emphasized his question, and Lou dropped the Winchester.

"Now what?" Lou asked. He looked to the woods where his partner had disappeared.

Justice walked forward, eyes cold and hard, and scooped up his hat. "Now I want to see Nathan Burbank, the mine manager," Justice answered. "When we get there, you can tell him that I'm working for Les Coyle." Which, strictly speaking, was true enough.

"Sure." Lou was eager to please now. "You should have said that before."

"It wouldn't have slowed Angel Farmer down any."

Justice picked up Lou's rifle and flung it away. Then he lifted the guard's handgun. "Have you got a horse?" he asked.

"No, we walk down."

"All right. Now you're going to walk up." Ruff recovered his buckskin horse, which eyed him dubiously, perhaps wondering what sort of madman it had gotten for an owner.

Justice swung aboard, his Spencer in hand, and they started toward the mine offices on the hill.

There was a hell of a lot of activity there. Mule-drawn wagons carrying lumber and supplies, steel bits, and hand tools rolled by. There were four shafts visible, and from each, iron carts were dumped down a long ore-littered slope. Below, men shoveled ore onto a conveyor belt leading to an iron tower. Somewhere the crusher itself was at work, breaking the stone down so that the gold could be retrieved in a mercury bath.

There were a lot of people around, and now some of them had begun to notice the tall man on the buckskin horse and his miserable-looking escort.

A buzz of comment coursed through the crowd, and two men started forward, but at a look from Justice they retreated a little way. At the mine office, a brick structure with two iron stovepipes poked through a solid-looking roof and two real glass windows, Ruff swung down.

"You don't need me, do you?" Lou asked.

"Sure I need you. Open the door and introduce me."

"It'll be the end of this job, mister," Lou said pleadingly.

"Tough. You weren't really cut out for it anyway, Lou," Justice said with mock sadness. Swallowing a curse, the guard opened the door to the office and Justice followed him into a tight, busy little area where two men in shirt-sleeves and a lady in a heavy, dark dress worked at all sorts of paperwork, barely looking up.

When they were finally noticed, things changed slightly. A tall man with a narrow mustache emerged from an inner office, a sheaf of papers in hand, and he stopped short.

"Lou? Damn you, what are you doing away from the gate—and who the hell's this?"

"A visitor," Lou managed to say before Justice stepped around him.

"The Duchess sent me up," Ruff Justice said. The tall man just watched him quietly, touching his thin mustache once with a long white finger.

"Did she? Fine. I'm sending you back."

"Mister Burbank—" Lou began.

"Get out of here! Get out and pick up your pay,"

Nathan Burbank ordered. Lou had been right about his chances of sticking to the job. But Ruff had trouble feeling sorry for him. "Howard, get two men down to the gate right now," Burbank said to another man, who spun away from his desk and took off as if it were a life-and-death matter. Ruff's eyes narrowed with amusement as he watched Burbank. He was cool and competent with the mannerisms and the look of a riverboat gambler rather than a mine boss.

"I assume," he said to Justice, "that I need *two* men down there. Angel Farmer wouldn't have let you come through voluntarily."

"No, he didn't. That's all right. I'm used to working my way around."

"You won't have to work your way *off* this property. We'll see that you have plenty of help."

"The Duchess might not like that."

"The hell with her. I knew her when she was Katie Price and I'll tell her that to her face."

"You might, but she still owns this place, doesn't she?"

"Yes, and she might fire me, but I really don't give a damn, Mister . . ."

"Justice."

"Mister Justice. I've got to run this place my way or not run it at all. If she sent you, go back and tell her you weren't welcome."

Ruff smiled. There wasn't much give in this brittle man. He couldn't help liking him in an undefined way—he had spine at least.

"The Duchess didn't send me," he told Burbank.

"Is that supposed to surprise me?" Nathan Burbank asked.

"No. I do have something we need to talk about, however. In private."

"I'm busy, Mister Justice, what is it?"

"Les Coyle's dead."

The mine manager just stared, his eyes expressionless. Then he nodded. "All right. Come into my office. Bill, don't let me be disturbed."

"No, Mister Burbank."

"Come on," Burbank snapped, and he led Justice into an inner room that smelled of tobacco and pine wood. He sat behind his desk in a green leather chair and lit a cigar. Waving out the match, he fixed his eyes on Ruff, who stood before him, rifle cradled in his arms.

"What is it, Justice? You say Les Coyle's dead. When? How?"

"Last night. Someone shot him at the Duchess's costume ball."

"But you don't know who."

"Some people thought it was Sal Campbell, but it wasn't," Ruff answered.

"Have you talked to Campbell?"

"It's kind of hard to talk to a dead man," Ruff said.

"I see. After Campbell, you don't have a guess."

"Maybe a guess or two."

"Why are you here, Justice?" Burbank leaned back and blew a fountain of blue smoke at the ceiling. Across his shoulder Ruff could look out the window and see gangs of miners moving around with wheelbarrows and sledges. "Why you, Justice, and not Jody Sharpe or Ty? Who are you anyway?"

"A friend of the Duchess. I was a friend of Les Coyle, too. That makes it my business."

"Maybe," Burbank acknowledged. "All right, why are you here? What's the Never-Never got to do with this? You think I did it, or Angel Farmer maybe?"

"I don't think you did it, no. If I had thought Farmer did it, he wouldn't be running loose in the woods right now; he'd be looking for a last resting place . . . or I'd be looking for him," Ruff said darkly.

"Then, what?"

"I'm looking for a reason Coyle was killed. I think there was a good one. When I stopped by the marshal's office this morning, it had been ransacked. Some papers were missing."

"What kind of papers?" Burbank suddenly looked wary.

"I was hoping you'd tell me. They were concerned with the Never-Never."

"They were, were they?" Burbank's cigar had gone out, but he didn't seem to notice.

"That's right. Someone stole them. Why?"

Burbank took a long while to answer. Outside, steel struck steel and someone shouted. The mine manager sighed. "I don't know why they were taken. There wasn't much in them. Nothing worth knowing. We hadn't gotten that far—or I hadn't. Maybe Les had stumbled over something."

"Something to do with the Never-Never."

"That's right. Well, it's no secret—we're being sabotaged, systematically, sadistically. We lost a boiler, we had a flooded shaft, we had a fire at the crusher. It's cost us a hell of a lot, Justice."

"Like?"

The manager lifted an eyebrow. "Like a million dollars and three lives."

"So someone has a grudge against the Never-Never."

"It looks like it, but I don't know who. Les had been following up on all the people I've discharged. And we're looking into the background of some of the others."

"Like Angel Farmer?"

Burbank flared up. "I know all about Farmer. He's violent and without scruples and personally I find him repugnant, but I wanted some tough men up here, the way things are. We're on the verge of closing down, and that's the truth. A mine that brings in five to six million a year on the verge of being closed by one maniac."

"Why do you say *one* man?"

"I don't know." Burbank became wary again. "It feels like one man."

"Someone has an idea?"

"We have a lot of ideas, tons of them," Burbank said. "Most generally it's held that the Ute's doing it."

"Why the Ute?"

"Figure it. He sold out for some trade whiskey, a few blankets, guns, knives, and beads."

"Where he came from, that's a fortune."

"Maybe. Maybe he got smart, maybe he got 'white eyes' and wants more. Maybe he's been told what the claim is really worth, and he figures if he can't have it, he'll see that we don't. He was always half-crazy anyway."

"You knew him?"

"Tanglefoot? Sure."

"That was his name?"

"Back then—the only name I ever heard. That was what McDowell called him anyway."

"You were around a long while back, then."

Burbank's eyes grew dark. "I told you so."

"And you knew Katie. Funny, I don't recall you. Although there was someone who looked like you dealing cards at Blue Boy Weaver's place, or am I wrong?"

Burbank didn't answer. His lips were tightly compressed. His hands, flat on the table, were white with the pressure he was putting on them.

"I don't remember you," Burbank said at last.

"No? Maybe because you were mostly drunk."

"Maybe," Burbank said without rancor. "I was mostly

drunk. Then I got up from the table, tossed the bottle aside, and went north, working with a pick and shovel for Tate Wiggins. Ten months later I was crew chief, and a year after that I was running the entire Sinkhole Mine. I worked my way up, Justice. And I like this a hell of a lot better than I liked a double-jack in a dark shaft. I like this a hell of a lot better than being drunk and dealing faro, understand me?"

"I understand you." It was hard not to believe him, too. The man was too passionate to be lying, or so it seemed. "Who besides the Ute could be doing this, then, Burbank?"

"Someone who wants the mine."

"What do you mean?"

"Someone who would be willing to take it off the Duchess's hands if she happened to get tired of it, tired of the trouble and killing."

"That would take some money."

"Backers wouldn't be hard to find."

"No? Not for a man who knew the game, I guess. Could you find backers, Burbank?"

That one stung, and the man came up an inch or two from his seat. "Yeah," he said, "I could find them. I could wreck this operation, make it unprofitable to run it. I could guarantee a good shelf of gold another fifty feet down, and I could retire wealthy. But I wouldn't do it."

"Who killed the Duke?"

The abruptness of the question from an unexpected quadrant stopped Burbank cold.

"How the hell would I know?"

"I just asked."

"I suppose that has something to do with this."

"I don't know. Maybe so."

"You don't believe a thing I've said, do you, Justice?" the mine boss asked.

"Help me to believe you."

"Just how do you propose that I do that?"

Justice walked to the window and stared out. The skies were graying over the mountains. The work went on, the hammering and chipping and grinding. "Let me take over where Les left off."

"Do what?" Burbank spun around in his chair and then rose to stand beside Justice. "Why should I?" he asked quietly. He thrust his hands into his pockets and waited for an answer.

"Because the mine's dying. You'll have to take the blame for it, won't you?"

"Maybe. I'll take the blame if I hire you on. Besides, we've got deputy marshals."

"I've met Jody and Ty. It's not a job for them."

"What qualifies you?"

"I'm hungry. I want Les Coyle's killer bad."

"I can't authorize it." Burbank wagged his head. At the same time he watched Justice almost hopefully. Maybe it was that important to Burbank to save the mine. As manager he was responsible for everything that had happened. He should have been able to stop it, to keep the mine at top capacity. "It would have to be the Duchess's decision," Nathan Burbank said.

"Don't worry about that. I'll see that Katie agrees to this."

"I don't like this," Burbank said. He looked Justice over.

"I know you don't."

"But I don't have much choice."

"No," Justice said, "you don't have any choice at all."

Burbank wasn't looking too chipper when Ruff left him. The mine boss stood in the door of the brick office staring at Justice as if he were watching a new kind of creature, and he looked relieved when Ruff mounted his horse and started down the hill.

"I'll be back in the morning," Justice said.

This parting message didn't appear to cheer Burbank any. He stood tight-lipped, hands in his pockets, watching Justice ride away before he turned and slammed the office door.

Justice rode past the two guards and continued on. He had another errand to run before he returned to Denver, and so he started his horse north up a narrow path between the ranks of trees, up an old mine road or Indian trail. Justice wasn't sure where it led, but it was going the direction he wanted to travel, and so he stayed with it, watching the clouds drift in darkly, listening to the distant thunder, seeing the trees begin to sway in the building wind.

As he rode, he thought, trying to make some sense out of a series of disconnected and random events. They didn't all fit, perhaps, but he had an idea that some of them did. Just how he couldn't puzzle out. The notions ran through his mind haphazardly. The Duke, who had worked for some European combine, was killed in the streets, while the Ute returned a prince to his squaws in the hills, and McDowell drank himself happily to death. The Delaney Street thugs had tried to run Coyle out of town. Blue Boy and Longden were tied up with Campbell, who was maybe tied up with the killer of Coyle, who had been investigating the sabotage at the Never-Never . . . Ruff felt like he had entered some never-never land himself. He been doing a lot of baseless bragging if he had given Burbank or anyone else the idea that he knew what was going on, that he was capable of solving everything, of finding Les' killer and setting the world right. . . .

Justice saw the brilliant muzzle flash from the trees,

and as he threw himself instinctively to one side, the bullet grazed his head and searing pain flooded his body. The buckskin was running up the trail, and Justice was falling down a long rocky bank, falling deeper into a different sort of never-never land, one where it was dark and painful and lonely.

7

When Ruff Justice opened his eyes, it was raining. He was on his back, staring up into the black and tumbling sky, and rain was hammering down. He tried to lift his head, but a flash of fire shot through his skull and he had to close his eyes and lie back. It wasn't real comfortable. His head was on a scattering of small rocks. One leg was bent under him, or he thought it was—it was numb, and he wasn't going to try lifting his head again to check it.

What had happened? he wondered.

He remembered a flash of orange-red lightning out of the dark woods and the simultaneous boom of thunder . . . A shot! He had been shot.

In that case the sniper might still be up there, looking for Justice, wanting to finish the job. It seemed as if Ruff had been lying there at the foot of the stony bluff for hours, possibly days, but it might have been only minutes. Minutes, while the ambusher figured out how to clamber down the rugged slope and put an end to Ruff Justice.

"Get up, damn you!" Justice told himself angrily, but

his body wasn't that easily intimidated. It twitched restlessly and then ever so slowly rolled over and uncoiled itself. That movement brought back the flaming pain in Ruff's skull, but there wasn't much he could do about it. Move and feel pain or lie there and never feel anything again.

He chose to move.

Ruff pulled his knees up and then rose. The rain was heavy now, slanting down steadily, washing over him. He was cold, shivering, his dark hair in his eyes. He reached for his belt gun and cursed when he found that it was gone. He looked upslope but couldn't see where it had fallen.

What he did see was the dark figure of the sniper with a rifle standing on a ledge halfway down the slope. Justice sprinted for the trees beyond just as a snap shot from the ambusher rang off stone near his feet and ricocheted into the darkness and rain.

Another bullet flew in Ruff's direction, but it was wild, slamming into the trunk of a huge pine tree, missing by yards.

Ruff stopped. He had to. He was nearly blind with pain from the head wound. He touched it, and when he pulled his hand away, it was smeared with blood.

"Bastard," Justice muttered. He was looking toward the bluff, a rage building in him. Someone had come to kill him, someone had come to take away the only life he would ever have, and it had been a quite enjoyable life at that, with orange sunsets and soft women and summer days in grassy fields and laughing friends. Now someone wanted to take it all away and lay him in a shallow, cold grave.

They couldn't do it; he wouldn't let them.

He didn't have time to worry about who it might be.

He thought of Angel Farmer first, but if it was Farmer, he was moving very fast for a man with a wounded leg.

The sniper was at the bottom of the bluff now. Ruff saw him crouch, touch something, maybe a patch of blood to see how much Ruff was bleeding, how long it would take the scout to curl up and die.

It wasn't enough. The would-be killer's head lifted toward the woods. He knew he was going to have to follow Justice in there and finish the job. Yet he was hesitant. Maybe he didn't know Ruff was unarmed.

He came forward, rifle leveled, moving slowly through the rain, and Justice pressed himself against the dark tree before him, drawing his bowie knife from the sheath at the back of his belt. Knives had a habit of not faring well against a rifle, but it was the only chance he had.

If only the pain behind his eyes would go away . . . The world wavered and blurred. The sniper looked like a dark, stalking ghost. Ruff blinked furiously but his eyes wouldn't clear. Cold rain dripped from the trees. The sniper moved silently across the pine needles.

Ruff Justice waited with his stag-handled bowie knife in hand.

The man crept nearer, and still Ruff couldn't see his face. It was as if the storm had darkened it, the rain washed it away.

"Angel Farmer," he muttered to himself. It had to be, didn't it? Maybe. Or how about Chase Longden or Harlon Staggs or Blue Boy, or . . . "Justice, you do make friends easily," he told himself dryly.

Except he might not be making any more. Ever.

Ruff didn't have a chance unless he let the man get on top of him, unless he allowed the stalker to come in hand-to-hand range, where the rifle would be of no advantage. There were certain risks implicit in that idea, but Ruff tried to dismiss them. Unsuccessfully.

He waited, pressed against the tree, knife cold and bright, water dripping from the polished, honed blade. He could hear nothing. There was only the rain, the moaning of the wind, as if somewhere the sky gods were weeping.

A footstep. Very soft.

Ruff waited, his ears straining, his vision still blurred. He had heard the one soft step and then nothing else. The sniper had stopped. How near? Had he seen Justice? The pine tree was wide, but maybe Ruff had given himself away.

Ruff let these ideas race around his mind frantically, going nowhere; then, without his willing it, they just seeped away. It wasn't important, no more than it was important who the sniper was. All that mattered was survival. Justice went cold and alert. The pain in his head seemed distant. It had returned, the old calmness, his old ally. That eerie calmness that sometimes came to him in battle, that was a trick of the organism desperate to survive, forcing itself to grow calm. Some men had it. They survived just a little longer.

Justice waited. He held the knife horizontally beside his hip, ready to slash, to kill. There was a second step now, less than a whisper, an almost inaudible sound. But it was loud enough to bring a smile to the lips of Ruff Justice.

Then he saw the front sight of the Winchester, the first inch of the long blue barrel, and his heart seemed to stop completely. The moment had come again.

The rifle muzzle moved. Ruff Justice grabbed it with his left hand and yanked, spinning from behind the tree and slashing up with the bowie knife. The cutting edge caught flesh, and blood flowed from a wrist. The sniper's head was thrown back with pain and anguish. He dropped the rifle and ran, leaving Justice with the Winchester and the bloody knife.

Ruff started after him.

He had some questions to ask, and he wanted to talk to the man before he bled to death—and that was what was going to happen. The bowie had bit deep.

A bullet rang off a tree near Ruff's head. The sniper, firing over his shoulder, ran on in panic. He didn't have a chance, but no one ever really believes that. He fired again, and Justice saw him stumble, saw him climb into a clump of rocks hidden in the trees. He climbed, he slipped and fell, dropping to the ground to lie still, staring up at the rain with pale eyes.

Justice had been running, or at least trying to run. Now his gait broke into a shambling trot. His mouth gaped open as he tried to breathe. The headache came back with brutal intensity. He stopped, took a slow breath, and walked on, finding the redheaded man still alive.

"Hello, Ed," Justice said to the man from Chase Longden's saloon. The sniper tried to spit at Justice but only blood came out.

"Killed him," Ed said.

"Who? Who killed who?" Justice crouched down in the rain.

"You killed him . . . brother."

"Sorry," Ruff said, although if his brother had died as a result of Justice's bullet, it was his own fault. He had come up with his weapon first. He had gone to work for Chase Longden with the idea of beating up people or shooting them as a way to make an easy living. But it hadn't been so easy. There wasn't any point in telling all that to Ed, who was getting set to follow his brother into whatever punk hell awaited them.

"You killed him."

"Did Longden send you?" Ruff asked. "Did you come because of your brother or did Longden send you? Did Longden order you to kill me?" The question trailed away. There wasn't any reason to expect a dead man to answer. Ruff stood, staggering a little as he did. He just looked at the redheaded gunman for a time, watching the rain fall on his face. Then he bent, picked up the man's handgun, and started on—where, he didn't know, but he had to get away from the stench of death.

He had killed and he wasn't proud of it. The man had begged for it. He had come looking. It was either Ruff or him. But none of that totally washed away the nausea Justice felt.

Nor did the rain, which hammered down, seeming to strike sparks inside Justice's skull with each raindrop. He became confused, not knowing which direction he was traveling. He couldn't see well at all, but he wasn't sure if it was because of settling darkness or that pain behind his eyes.

In his haze, he nearly walked into a bent oak tree. He stopped and squatted down, trying to catch his breath. Then he was on his side, lying there while someone beat steadily at his temple with a little red hatchet.

The rain was endless, but it became warmer and then downright hot as a sparking drop touched his hand. Ruff opened his eye and stared at the fountain in front of his face. It was red and gold and glowing, very nice, very lovely. But difficult to see how they could color the water like that. Make it warm.

There was a face beyond the fountain, which had altered and become flames, hot dancing flames. The face was dark and narrow and hung with twisted gray hair.

"So you return from the journey to the dark land," a voice from somewhere said, and Justice tried to puzzle it out. Who or what was making the sound so like human speech?

He tried sitting up. It was easier to think that way. Bracing himself, he got up and sat holding his head for a long while, staring at his feet.

He heard water trickling, heard distant thunder, but he wasn't outside. He was in a low cave. Rain had glossed the wall of stone opposite him. It was a cold and damp place. Ruff was staring at a fire, and beyond the fire the face slowly came into focus.

"Can't see too well," Ruff apologized. "Took a knock on the head. Fell onto some rocks."

"Bad knock," the voice answered.

Ruff peered at the man, who was poking at the fire with a crooked stick. He was Indian, Ute, Ruff guessed. "Tanglefoot?" he asked slowly.

The Ute grinned. "You know me, but I do not know you. Has my fame traveled far?"

"It was just a guess. They said you were around here."

"Yes, just Tanglefoot. I am around here."

"Not with your people."

"No." The voice was heavy. "Not there."

Ruff felt a bowl placed in his hand. It was warm, and when he dipped into it with the horn spoon, he found venison and corn stew, very tasty, and he went at it eagerly as the rain pounded down in the blackness beyond the mouth of the cave.

"Can they see that fire?" Ruff asked.

"No. Very much willow trees in front of the cave. Why do they hunt you, tall man?"

"I don't know. I just don't know."

"Maybe friends of the man you killed?" Tanglefoot asked slyly.

"Maybe." He handed the bowl back, and it was filled again. Ruff finished that off in silence. When it was empty, he was full and feeling much better. He touched his scalp gingerly and found that a poultice had been applied to his wound.

"That takes the poison out," the Indian said. "Mistletoe and wild rice. Very good."

"Thanks, Tanglefoot. It seems I owe you now."

"I let no one die," Tanglefoot said, slightly offended. "I saw the dead man. I saw you. Was it a good fight?"

The old man's eyes were fire-bright now, excited by memories of past battles perhaps. He yearned to spend the night around the campfires of his people in a safe and warm lodge, telling war stories. For some reason he was alone out here. He looked to Ruff for entertainment.

"It was a good fight," Justice said in the Ute tongue, something that seemed not to surprise Tanglefoot at all. Then Justice went on to tell the story, not briefly or matter-of-factly, as he would have told a white audience, but much embellished, reliving each breath to make it a story worth telling. When he was through, Tanglefoot nodded.

"You killed his brother. He had to come to you. Honor demanded it."

"Maybe. These brothers, though, had more greed than honor."

"Perhaps this is so with these white men, I do not know," the Indian said, prodding the fire to life again.

"What are you hiding from?" Ruff asked.

"Hiding? Why should I hide?"

"I don't know. Maybe because the miners are looking for you, the white lawmen."

"Looking for me?" Tanglefoot asked.

"Yes, didn't you know?"

"How could I know? What miners? The Never-Never?" The Ute seemed perplexed.

"Yes, that's right."

"What have I to do with that? Years ago I sold my part of the mine. McDowell and me. We found it, but we both were tired of digging holes. McDowell said, 'Let us take some money and spend it while we are still strong men. Let us find women and drink whiskey and eat honey.' To me this seemed good counsel. I too was tired of digging, of being away from my people."

"They think maybe you got tired of being with your people, that you decided you hadn't been paid enough, that you were angry with the miners for cheating you."

"The Duke did not cheat."

"You knew the Duke?"

"Yes, he paid what I asked. How can I come back and say I want more?"

"They think maybe you got hungry for money."

"For money—what good does that do me? I was wealthy and it did not make me happy. I went to my people and took two wives, sisters, young and pretty. I sat in my lodge and smoked good tobacco and gave gifts to all my friends."

"What happened?"

"A man who was my friend took my wives. He took my beads and gifts, my good tobacco and my new rifle, and together they ran away. While I was digging holes, he had wanted my wives. He had courted them but had no gifts to give. They planned it all together. They robbed me and went away in the dark of the night."

"What did you do?" Ruff asked.

The old man lifted his fire-painted face. "What could I do? He had stolen. They had gone with him."

Ruff nodded. What could Tanglefoot have done but track them down and kill the three of them? It was what honor demanded. Yet he couldn't have been welcome with his people after that.

"The money didn't do you much good, did it?"

"It was bad money," Tanglefoot said. There was something behind his words. Ruff watched the old Ute's face closely, reading fear, or at least what he thought was fear.

"Why?" The fire wavered. A gust of wind touched it, and it moved and spun.

"Do you not know yet?" Tanglefoot asked, his face somber and dark. "The Never-Never. It is a bad place, a spirit place. It was dug wrong, without ceremony, and so it opened up the place where the dark things underground dwelled." The fire shifted again, and this time Ruff too felt the chill of the breeze as it touched his spine.

"What do you mean, Tanglefoot? What are you saying?" Justice asked. He could hear the wind moaning and chanting; the old man went on.

"Death comes from Never-Never. The dark things in the earth guard it. Look back, tall man. First was McDowell who died. He opened the mine. Second was the Duke. He bought the mine. Third, my wives, my friend, touched by dark spirits. Then two redhaired men. The marshal, your friend you spoke of. You did not die, but you would have without Tanglefoot."

It was quite a list, not even counting the three miners and Sal Campbell. But Ruff Justice had a different idea of the dark spirit that haunted the Never-Never. It was called Gold and it wormed its way into men's hearts and made them greedy, made them grasping, made them willing to kill. It was an ancient and powerful god, and if there was a malevolent spirit in the Never-Never, Gold was it.

Still, as the fire burned low and the wind shrieked and the rain fell down outside the dark cavern, it was easy enough to believe in Tanglefoot's cave creatures, the dark spirits who lived underground.

Justice didn't sleep well that night.

8

Tanglefoot was up hours before Justice. He had a fire going, and over it three woodcocks were roasting. Justice sat up, still suffering from a headache, but feeling alert and strong. His vision had cleared. Tanglefoot was smiling. Ruff could see where McDowell would have found the Ute a good companion.

"You sleep late."

"I had to sleep some of the poison out, I think," Justice answered.

"Your horse, tall man, it has only half a tail?"

"That's right. A buckskin with its tail cropped."

"Yes. I have it for you. Also a long gun . . . the sheath it is in, was it made by Cheyenne Indian hands?"

"Crow Indians," Justice answered.

"Crow, yes." Tanglefoot cocked his head, thinking silently on that for a while. "I found this dead man's horse, but I turned it loose. If I ride it, they will say I shot him."

"Have you got a horse?"

"No. It is better for me not to have one," Tanglefoot said seriously. "I have enemies everywhere, it seems."

"And one friend. A good friend. Tanglefoot, will you help me?"

"You are still sick?"

"Not that. I want to find out what's happening at the Never-Never. I want to find out who's been sabotaging the mine and why, because I think whoever it is killed my friend, Les Coyle. In my bones, I'm sure of it."

"Yes?" Tanglefoot was cautious.

"I'm going to return to the mine. Not this morning, but soon. I'm going to go inside if I have to, and I'm going to sleep there if I have to. I'm going to catch this man. But I can't be everywhere. If you could be outside watching, from the forest, you could help me."

"I do not know. It is a bad place."

"Yes, it's a bad place."

"I do not have to go in it?"

"No, Tanglefoot, not inside—that's my part of the deal."

"I do not know." He was undecided and Ruff didn't press it. He would have offered him money, but it might have insulted Tanglefoot. Anyway the Ute seemed to have no use for it. Ruff had been hoping Tanglefoot might do it for the adventure, but he was frightened of his spirits, very frightened.

"Do what you must, Tanglefoot." Justice rose, feeling only a little dizzy. "I have to be going now. I'll be around the mine until this is solved—or until the bad luck of the Never-Never hits me too. You'll be able to contact me somehow if you decide to do this."

"Yes." Tanglefoot was somber again for a minute, then he brightened, rose, and grinning, stuck out his hand.

The two men went out into the sunlight, and there stood the buckskin in the willows, looking as good as new. Ruff's gear had been stowed beneath a flat rock, and the Ute gave it to him, the Spencer included.

Then Justice saddled up and swung aboard. Before he rode out, he said, "Think on it, Tanglefoot. I can use your help."

"Yes, yes, I will." The Ute added silently as Justice rode on, "Be careful, tall man. Be careful of those dark spirits. I think they wait for you somewhere."

The day was bright, a few gray clouds clinging to the sides of the high peaks where some new snow had fallen during the night. The air was clean and cold. In the meadows the grass was tall and green, turning silver when the wind blew. There were icy little rills everywhere, winding their way across the meadows where mushrooms of pink and violet and blue flourished.

Ruff saw a good-sized herd of elk led by a massive buck carrying a rack like an oak tree. Beyond the meadow he found a spruce forest with a large pocket of golden aspen clinging to the side of a white cliff to the north. He rode the buckskin down along the wooded slope, crossed the narrow silver river in the bottom, and entered the dark canyon.

It was a pretty little place, isolated but appealing. Cedar and spruce flourished and there was good grass in a narrow band along the bottom. The bluffs rose high, timbered and twisted. Beyond the bluffs the high mountains, aloof, snow-streaked, were visible.

"Les, you would have liked it here. I can see that." Colson Canyon was a place a man could live out his days happily.

The little white house came into view as Justice rounded a bend in the canyon bottom. The river, which had been flowing smooth and silent, quick as mercury, hit a jumble of rocks here and briefly frothed and hissed and bawled at Ruff. But beyond the rocks it slowed again, broadened, and fanned out to water the graze. The house overlooked it all. It should have been a cheerful, bright, clean little place with its white walls and green roof and shutters, but it looked only dismal, small, and neglected, like some pretty bauble lost in the wilderness.

Ruff walked the buckskin toward the house, seeing the yellow curtains in the windows now, curtains Lily had sewn and hung, maybe humming as she worked, thinking the kinds of thoughts women about to marry think, stopping now and then to smile secretly or clutch the curtains to her breast.

There was a buggy beside the house. It wasn't new, but the green wheels had been freshly painted. More of Les' work probably. There were two horses in the pasture behind the house as well, so someone was there.

Ruff swung down and went to the door.

He rapped twice, three times, but nothing happened. He had turned his back on the door and started around toward the back before it finally opened and Lily Sly stood there, blond, pale, and tiny.

"Ruff Justice!" she cried.

"Hello, Lily."

"What's happened to you? You look awful."

"That's more or less natural," Ruff said. "I got a knock on the head, that's all. Everything's all right now."

"It is, is it?" she said, putting her hands on her hips as if she were going to brook no nonsense. "What's that tied on there? Some bag of weeds or such? Indian cures are for Indians, Ruff. You come in here and sit down and let me look at that. A little lye soap and some carbolic first, and then we'll see what's to be done."

"Lily . . ." Ruff tried to object, but it did no good. The blonde took his arm above the elbow and steered him into the house, which didn't have a lot of furniture, but did have a braided rug in front of the fireplace and a rocker beside that. There was a basket with knitting in it on the chair.

The kitchen had a hand-hewn puncheon table and four chairs, a brand-new black iron stove, and some half-finished cupboards. Lily guided Ruff to one of the chairs.

"Sit down, Mister Justice. Right there."

"Yes, ma'am," he said, smiling.

"It's not funny. I'll have a look at that, and you tell me what's brought you all this way and how you happened to knock yourself on the head."

"I came out here," Ruff said, not missing the irony, "to see if you needed some help."

"Help?" The hands faltered for just a moment, then went on, deftly dabbing carbolic on the scalp wound. "Why would *I* need help?"

"Because you're alone in a lonesome place. You've had it pretty rough. I didn't see any firewood by the fireplace for one thing. Have you got any cut?"

"I don't know. Les . . ." Her voice dropped off into a hopeless abyss.

"I'll get to that later, then. Ouch!"

"Burns, doesn't it? I thought you could take pain, though, Mister Justice."

"Me? Not much better than anyone else, I don't suppose. I sure don't care for it."

"No, neither do I." Lily's voice drifted off somewhere again. Her hand, resting on Ruff's shoulder, gave him a gentle squeeze, whether it was gratitude or absentmindedness or a simple muscular contraction, Justice didn't know. He could smell her little-girl scent—strong soap and vanilla—and beneath it the beginnings of womanhood. She moved across the room, putting the carbolic in the pantry.

"How was Cousin Katie?" she asked.

"Who? Oh, I forgot you were related to the Duchess. She was fine when I last saw her. That's been a while."

"I thought you had just ridden out from town." Lily wiped her hands on her plaid apron and came to sit across the table from Ruff.

"No. I was out at the Never-Never."

"At the mine?" she asked, her blue-gray eyes widening. "What ever for?"

"Just looking into something for Katie," he answered. He avoided mentioning that Les had been doing the same thing and had gotten killed for it.

"Oh . . ." If she had heard him, Ruff couldn't tell by looking at her. Perhaps she hadn't time to think of other people's affairs just now. "Well"—the smile was brave but weak as she came to her feet—"if you really wouldn't mind splitting some of that wood out there, I'll show you where Le—I keep the ax."

"Fine." Ruff stood, scratching at his scalp just below the wound. It itched like crazy now.

Outside, the sky was bright and clear, but there were clouds beginning to mass in the northern skies. The valley was in shadow already as the sun dropped toward the Rockies. Ruff was led to the woodshed and shown the bucksaw and ax, maul and sawhorse. Everything was well-used but well-cared-for, the handles treated with linseed oil, the tools carefully stowed away. Les had been a careful man. Except for that last time, but then, how could he have expected to get it there?

Ruff got to work, and Lily, after a moment's hesitation, went away, leaving him to it. After half an hour Justice was warm, despite the chill in the air, and he peeled off his shirt before getting back to work, rhythmically sawing the logs Les had brought in from the uplands.

Les again. Les was gone, but everything on the place showed his handiwork. He had left his mark. It would be hard for the woman to forget him. This was, after all, to have been their honeymoon cottage.

It was hard for Ruff to forget too. Les was dead and it may not have been Les they wanted. Justice thought it was; in his guts he felt that it was the marshal they intended to get, but there was that possibility that it was Ruff they had tried to kill. Ruff, who had been wearing that costume Les was killed in.

He worked on and the day passed with amazing quickness. The stack of wood in the shed was slowly mounting.

"Would you like some water, Ruff?"

Justice turned, to find that Lily had come back. She had changed to a yellow dress and had brushed her hair, tying a yellow ribbon in it. She looked quite pretty and not so very young.

"Yes. Thanks."

"It's hard work, isn't it?" she asked, giving Justice a wooden cup while she waited, holding the pitcher.

"It's not my favorite," Justice told her, looking at his hand. "I've found a couple new places to get blisters."

"You've done enough for today," she said.

"Maybe. But winter's coming on. Who'll cut the rest of it for you?"

"I don't know . . ." A little despair had begun to creep into her voice. "I'm so far away from everything out here, from everyone. It's a lonesome place. It would have been all right with Les, but what is there to do by myself? At night I hear wolves and strange noises. When it storms down this canyon, it's just terrible. I never see anyone. Town is miles away . . ." She stopped short. "Sorry. It's my concern and not yours."

"That's right. But I'm a friend of yours. Friends should share concerns."

"Thank you."

"For what?"

"For saying you're my friend." Her hand briefly touched his arm, her eyes briefly met his.

"Have you thought of living with Katie? I know she wouldn't mind. She's got a lot of room."

"She asked. I said no," Lily answered with determination, pursing her lips.

"Why?"

"I don't know. It didn't seem right. The poor relation going to the rich cousin's house to live off of her."

"Katie wouldn't look at it that way."

"But I do. I would like a house like that, but it would have to be mine. I'd like everything she has, but I don't want to beg for it or borrow it. Well." She shrugged. "I'll hire a man to do the rest of the wood, Ruff. You've done plenty and it's nearly dark anyway."

It was at that. The shadows had gone to deep blue and the bluffs were purple above them. Justice put on his shirt, feeling Lily's eyes on him.

"I'll take an armload or two in for you before I go," he offered.

"All right. Yes . . ." Lily was off in the distances again. Justice found himself worrying about the girl. Her mind didn't seem just right to Justice, not yet. He didn't like the way her eyes focused and then unfocused, shifting from uncertain point to uncertain point, nor the way her voice too frequently trailed off. The woman was having a heavy going of it. He almost wished he'd sent the doctor out to have a look at her, though what Doc could have done he had no idea.

He tramped into the house with the second load of firewood just as the skies caught fire and blazed briefly with crimson flame before the fire went out and a few orange-gold embers glowed softly in the western mountains. It was going to be a long ride in the darkness back to town.

Ruff stacked the wood by the fireplace and stood dusting his hands. The kitchen door opened and Lily said, "You come and get it, Ruff Justice."

She had a wooden spoon in her hand and a smile on her lips. Ruff shook his head. "I've got to be going, Lily."

"You're not going out on the trail until I've fed you, mister. You need something warm in you. You worked hard today, now you come and sit before I get good and mad."

"All right," he answered with a smile. "I wouldn't want to see you mad. Just show me where to wash up."

She provided a basin and pitcher, a clean towel, and a bar of strong soap. This was all placed on the bureau in her small room. Bare logs formed the walls. The bed was wooden, sturdy, carved, well-used. A marshal didn't make much money. The room was a far cry from Katie Price's luxurious bedroom. Yet it could have made a cozy place. Many men would have wanted nothing more than a good bed and a place to sit down before the fire. Many women would have no doubt traded places with Lily Sly—two nights ago.

Now the place was empty and cold and just a little drab. Ruff washed up the best he could, hearing Lily in the kitchen, making pleasant dinnertime sounds, humming a little.

Dinner was white beans with a ham hock boiled in for flavor, and hot corn bread. It was good, filling, and there was plenty of it.

"I guess it's not like Katie's meals," Lily said.

Ruff looked across the table to see the blonde, hands clasped beneath her chin, watching him eat. "No. But it's good. It's cooking to please a man. I felt just a little embarrassed eating some of Katie's delicacies."

"Did you really?" There was some astonishment in Lily's voice.

"Yes, I did."

She cocked her head in wonder, nodded, and rose to go to the black iron stove, where coffee had been boiling. She took a cloth and folded it around the handle and then poured, serving it hot and black and strong to Ruff. She was in the act of pouring when the thunder rumbled distantly.

"Damn," Justice said.

"Will it rain?" she asked with something close to fear in her voice.

"Afraid so. Sounds like it's fixing to bluster. You don't have a man's hat around, do you? I've got my rain slicker, but I lost my hat somewhere."

She shook her head. She was standing, listening as if for approaching doom. When the thunder growled again, close at hand, she nearly dropped the coffeepot.

Ruff stood and put his arm around her. "Steady, Lily."

"It's my nerves. It's been so hard, and out here—"

Lightning painted a brilliant white picture in the window frame, and thunder cannonaded close enough to shake the mountain cabin. Lily screamed and dropped the pot. She stood there shaking, stamping her feet. Then she looked at Ruff Justice and fainted dead away.

The rains came down.

Ruff scooped the woman up. There were coffee stains on her new yellow dress. Her hair ribbon had slipped loose, and her yellow hair fell free in luxurious profusion. She was light in Ruff's arms, light and soft and small, and he carried her to her bedroom and placed her on the bed. Thunder crashed again and Ruff scowled.

She stirred a little, her arm going across her face protectively. Justice unbuttoned her tiny shoes and threw a quilt over her. The rain fell like gravel, hammering the roof of the small house. The wind had begun to creak and whine in the eaves. Lily's eyes flickered open—wide, pain-filled eyes.

"You won't leave me, will you, Ruffin? Not tonight?"

"No," he promised. "I won't leave you tonight."

9

After getting her to sleep, Justice walked to the front door. Opening it, he was met by a wash of rain and cold wind. Lightning danced across the skies. The dark peaks revealed themselves starkly and then pulled the dark draperies of cloud and night in front of them. Thunder rolled down the long valley. It would have been a fine night for Les to cozy up to his new bride, but it was a hell of a night for a woman alone, one who carried all that grief.

He closed the door, barred it, and went into the front room. There he had thrown a couple of blankets on the floor before the fireplace. Justice split some kindling with his bowie knife and placed some bigger sticks on top of that. From the still-burning kitchen stove he retrieved a smoldering brand, and placed it against the kindling. Puffing gently, he breathed life into the dead wood, and the new fire sparked and curled smoke, and the tiny flames grew.

Then he rose, looking around for a way to make himself more comfortable. The floor would be hard and cold.

He decided on the chair, and taking off his gunbelt and boots, he settled into the rocker, tugging the blankets up to his chin. There he fell asleep while the storm ranted on, threatening and blustering.

When he awoke, the fire was burning low. The room was still warm, very warm—the house was tightly built.

The woman, dressed in a sheer nightgown, stood before the fire. Her blond hair tumbled down across her breasts. Her body, seen clearly through the thin material of her gown, was young and healthy and rounded.

"Lily?" Ruff was half-asleep, and she seemed a thing out of a dream. She didn't answer, but she came to him and sat at his feet, and her hand slipped under the blanket to search for his manhood.

"I'm afraid," she murmured, her cheek against his thigh now. "Afraid and lonely and maybe desperate. I think I shall scream if I have to be alone any longer. Don't make me be alone." She looked up, her hand gripping him tightly, urging his shaft to life.

"Lily, it's no good this way."

"It is good. Good for me. I want you in my bed. I want to touch you and take you in me. I want you to rock against me and find pleasure and then lie with me, warming me, keeping the night away."

He could have refused her touch, the hands that crawled over him, rubbing him, promising more, but he couldn't refuse the pleading of her eyes, the need in her voice. It hurt no one. Les was gone. He couldn't offer her this kind of comfort.

Besides, she was beautiful and young and soft; there was no denying it.

Ruff rose from the chair, and before the fire he stripped off his clothes. Lily watched him anxiously, lifting her nightdress over her head. She dropped it onto the blankets already strewn on the hearth, and that became their bed.

"Lie down," she said, "please."

Ruff got down on his back and Lily, starting with his forehead, worked her way down across his body, administering small kisses as she went. Her blond hair trailed across Ruff's chest and abdomen as her mouth touched his flesh, bringing a chilling sensation to his fire-warmed body.

She reached his groin, and Ruff heard her sigh with pleasure as she hefted him, measuring him with her fingertips, which slid down his erection to his sack. Then Lily lifted her leg up and over and straddled Ruff Justice, facing his feet.

He reached up and rubbed her back, letting his finger trail down her spine to its very base, sending a tingle of excitement through her. She was warm and damp sitting across him, and when she bent low to kiss his inner thighs, her hair was like soft rain caressing his flesh. He sat half up and nipped at her buttocks, reaching around to cup her full breast with one hand while the other slowly spread Lily, a finger dipping inside to toy with her.

She turned suddenly. Her eyes were wide with sensuality and need. She lifted herself and placed the head of his shaft to her soft inner flesh. She rubbed herself with it for a time, her head lolling back, her mouth open, both of her hands on Ruff's erection, ever so gently stroking it before she lurched forward and Ruff slid in to the hilt.

Lily sagged against him, her breasts against his chest, her mouth searching frantically for his, finding it hungrily. Ruff lay still, but his body was having none of that. She was young and eager and there was rain washing down outside. The fire was warm and her lips encouraging.

He arched his back slightly and she moaned, her body responding instantly with its own small movements, which became a swaying, rocking need.

She lifted herself again, and Ruff had to crane his neck to find her breasts with his lips, taking her tender nipples into his mouth while Lily's body convulsed and, with a hard spasm, found a damp and violent climax that sent her pitching against him, her pelvis bruising his as she breathed raggedly in and out. Small birdlike noises of concentration escaped her full lips before a second violent climax washed over her and she cried out with joy moments before Ruff's responding completion filled her with his answering satisfaction, deep and draining.

He lay back then, stroking her soft back, the silky contours of her firm young ass, feeling her light kisses and the lingering warmth of her body. And then she was asleep, breathing softly, faintly snoring, her blond hair across Ruff's face and shoulders, her eyelid fluttering against his chest.

Justice reached out, grabbed a blanket to wrap around them, and fell asleep while the fire burned low. It was a shallow, troubled sleep with many dreams and many problems that the logic of dreams could not solve.

Lily wasn't there when he awoke. How she had drawn away from him, dressed, and left without waking him was a mystery. Ruff Justice was no heavy sleeper.

But she was gone. There was bread on the table and cheese, and an apple.

And the note:

Thank you, Ruff Justice. For feeling sorry for a woman alone. This morning would have been too difficult.

"She was right," Justice muttered. "It would have been difficult indeed."

With a kitchen knife he sawed off a chunk of bread and cut a wedge of cheese. Then he finished dressing, opening the door as he did to look out at the empty meadow and the clear skies above the mountains.

He had saved the apple for the buckskin, and he fed it to him before slipping the bit into his mouth, saddling and riding out of the little ranch. The buggy was gone, and both of the other horses. She was gone, and Justice doubted he would see her again.

"That too would be difficult," he said aloud. The buckskin twitched an ear but did not respond. It had matters other than human romance on its mind.

Denver was a rowdy, rambling place, the mud deep in its streets, the gambling and drinking on Delaney Street continuing unabated when Ruff Justice rode in again. He saw Jody Sharpe as he walked his horse up Grand, and the deputy turned expectantly toward him. But Ruff Justice only lifted a hand and rode on by, the buckskin hock-deep in red mud.

The big house was cold-looking despite the smoke from two of its chimneys. Ruff rode up the gravel driveway and swung down beneath the great white oak tree. He walked up the steps and turned the doorbell key. Harlon Staggs, big and ugly, wearing his too-tight butler's uniform, answered the door.

"Yes, sir?"

"Katie here?" Ruff asked.

"I shall inquire, sir," Staggs answered. You had to hand it to the former bouncer and hired thug; he was trying. If only he didn't speak as if he had a mouthful of gravel and walk like an ape.

Justice waited in the open doorway, seeing the polished floors inside, the gilt-framed paintings, the carpeted staircase. In a minute Katie was there, sweeping toward him in a long green dressing gown with ruffles everywhere.

"Where in God's name have you been, Ruff Justice? Don't you think a person worries about you? The day before yesterday you headed out for the Never-Never. You didn't come back. I thought they'd thrown you down a shaft or cut your head off or shot you—"

"Who?"

"What?" Katie was taken aback. Her stream of complaints stopped abruptly.

"*Who* did you think did all these things, Katie?"

"Hell, I don't know." She shrugged. "Come in, quit standing on the porch, the neighbors will talk. Whoever does those things, I guess, whoever is trying to wreck the mine."

"That's what I mean to find out."

"You're not going to tell me where you were, are you?" Katie said, refusing to let go of her train of conversation.

"Trying to find out. Listen, Katie. I went out to the Never-Never. I talked to Nathan Burbank. He doesn't like the idea much, but he's willing to let me investigate up there, to poke around and find out who's trying to kill the twenty-million-dollar golden goose. *That* is what Les was doing when he was killed. I need your permission as well, I suppose."

"No!"

"What?"

"No," she said, flatly this time. She folded her arms and shook her head, and those green eyes of the Duchess of Denver were firm with resolution.

"Look, Katie—"

"No. Damn you, Justice. You just hypothesized that Les was killed because he looked too deeply into this thing. That ought to give you a clue that it may be dangerous. I won't have you killed over the Never-Never.

I've got further use for you, mister. You already went out there and you've already been hurt, haven't you? What's that on your head? It's no golden-goose egg. Looks more like a lump on the head, and I'll lay you odds you got it at the Never-Never."

"I didn't, as a matter of fact."

"I'll bet. And you were gone two days. What were you doing, investigating? Or laying hurt up some canyon in the rain?"

"Katie, I *need* to do this, do you understand?"

"Because Les was your friend."

"That's right."

"What about me, Justice?" She touched her breasts.

"I need to do it, Katie."

"Oh, Christ. All right! What do I care? I'll give you a letter."

"Now that that's settled," Ruff said, and he gathered the Duchess in his arms and held her close. Her nose wrinkled up slightly.

"Lye soap. Carbolic," she mumbled.

"What?"

"I take it back. You weren't laying up some canyon, were you? What were you doing, Ruff?" She had her hands on his chest and now she pushed away a little.

"An old prospector found me," Ruff said.

"Sure. Which old prospector?"

"Tanglefoot," Justice said.

"You're kidding."

"Not at all," he answered.

"Well, you're not telling all the truth, then. Don't forget, I know Tanglefoot, and if he ever used soap in his life, it was before he came to live with Willy McDowell up in those hills." Katie shook her head, studying his blue eyes, that lean, smiling face. "Don't know why I care for you the way I do, Justice," she said. "Come on, I'll give you your letter of authorization."

They walked toward the library. A blur of movement upstairs along the landing caught Ruff's eye, and he was in time to see the blonde in the yellow dress vanish into an upstairs bedroom.

"Lily Sly?"

"Yes. She was in town. I practically forced her to accept my invitation this time. She needs to stay around people. What's the matter, Justice, don't you think it was a good idea?"

"No," he answered, "it's fine, just fine." But he was frowning when he started toward the library door again, following in the wake of the lilac-scented Duchess.

She sat at the desk and began scratching out a letter. "If you get yourself killed doing this, Ruff, I'll never forgive you," she said, folding it and handing it to him.

"I don't mean to." Ruff placed the letter in his shirt. "Katie . . . ?"

"Yes?" She rose behind the desk and Ruff's eyes went briefly to the cleavage revealed by the parted dressing gown. She saw his look and smiled. "There was something you wanted to do—with me?"

"I'd like to, but not now. I wanted to ask you. This corporation your husband worked for. Have they just given up on the Never-Never?"

Her face paled and her mouth drew down a little. "Who have you been talking to?"

"No one. I just wanted to know."

"All right . . ." She breathed in sharply, the breath hissing past her teeth. "They've filed a new suit with the state superior court. They say they still have a claim, that the Duke was acting as their agent and had no right to purchase the property for himself."

"Can they win?"

"I'm not a lawyer, Ruff."

"But you have one."

Katie was silent for a minute. Her eyes sparkled. "Yes, I have one. He doesn't know. Maybe they can get the mine back. Maybe they can get what I've already made . . . and spent."

"Where does that put you?"

"Delaney Street, where do you think, Justice?" Katie shrugged. "I don't suppose it would really matter. I've had my fling. I've run a saloon before, I could do it again."

"What would happen if the mine were destroyed? Would they drop the suit, figuring it wasn't worthwhile?"

Her lips were compressed into a straight line. There was a glitter of anger in her eyes. "I wouldn't know. You think I want to do that, Ruff, that that gives me a reason to kill men, to destroy my own property?"

"I don't know, Kate. I swear I don't. I only know this: someone's got a reason, and he kills for it."

"Me . . . ?" She was red-hot, but Justice reached for her nevertheless. She fought back, but he pulled her into his arms, forced a kiss on her, and held her until she accepted it, until she was hungry for more.

"We have an appointment for later," he said. "There's something, after all, that I wanted to do with you."

"Me too." She hung her head a little. "Hard times, Ruff, hard times. Make it all better for me."

"I'll do my best," he promised. He kissed her again and then walked toward the front door past a scowling Harlon Staggs. The Duchess of Denver was in the doorway, wearing that flouncy green gown, lovely and summoning, when Justice swung aboard that bobtailed buckskin and rode out. The other lady was framed in an upstairs window. Justice saw her there, watching. He had just a peek at Lily Sly peering from the curtained window, thinking who knew what, perhaps that death would come again. They all believed it. They all believed in the dark underground demons of Tanglefoot. Maybe they were all smarter than he was.

He stopped by the marshal's office, but only Ty Roosevelt was there, and the bald deputy couldn't tell him of any progress at their end of the investigation.

"Jody tried to talk up Blue Boy Weaver, but Blue Boy can't be talked up."

"Talked up?"

Ty Roosevelt blinked. "Why, Jody tells him what we got on him and how close he is to being brought to court and maybe Blue Boy gives him something on Les Coyle's murder—that's the way it works. But Blue Boy won't be talked up on this."

"Does Jody think he knows something?"

"Blue Boy knows something about everything, but Blue Boy's been at his trade a long while and he won't talk unless he has a motive."

"I'd think staying out of court would be a motive," Ruff suggested.

"Maybe. He wanted to trade off with Jody there."

"What did he want to trade off?"

Ty suddenly looked sly. "You'd like to know?"

"No, I'm standing here to see if the buffalo hunting's any good," Justice said, peeved.

"Don't need to get testy," Ty complained. "It's like this: Blue Boy says he don't know a thing about the killing of the marshal, which is likely a lie, but Jody knows he can't crack him. Jody says he's going to run him in for selling opium to the Chinee folks, which he could do anytime he wanted. Blue Boy says, 'Now, wait a minute, Deputy, I got something you might want to hear. Trade me off.'"

"And Jody did," Ruff said, growing impatient. "What was it, Ty?"

Ty smiled crookedly. "Just this: there's a price on your head, Justice."

"A price on my head? What are you talking about?"

"A price. Five hundred gold dollars. Chase Longden put it there. You broke his wrist and shot one of his boys up, showed him up in his own place. Oh, there's nothing written down or anything that could be pinned on Longden, but the word's out to all the thugs and gun-carrying scum that you're fair game."

"I see," Justice said. That explained the ambush in the forest, perhaps. The redhead would have jumped at a chance to make five hundred dollars and get his revenge as well.

"We can't do anything about it, you know," Ty said, not seeming unhappy about it. "I mean, we've got nothing on Chase, and say we bring him in, the bounty's still good, isn't it?"

Ruff Justice said he supposed it was, and Ty warned him. "Then, you be careful. You just be awful careful. Anyone out there with a gun could be your man. Anyone at all."

10

Denver had always been a lucky town for Ruff, but it wasn't going to be on this trip, and he was glad to turn his back on it and ride into the mountains once again, toward the Never-Never.

He hadn't shown it in town, but he was uneasy. It doesn't do your nerves any good to know that any stranger might be wishing to gun you down for a handful of gold. He had been tempted to go over and finish Longden off, but that would put him in the wrong. Besides some drunk with big ideas would most likely have cut him down the minute he walked through the door.

The mountains were clean, the air sweet and cold, and Ruff drank it in as he rode through the deep, dark ranks of the spruce trees into the high country.

The guards at the gate were a little more hospitable than Angel Farmer and his sidekick had been. Still they eyed him suspiciously and Justice was told, "I got to escort you up to the office."

"Fine, let's go."

"No guns."

Ruff handed them over. He didn't care for the idea, but he could understand the reason behind the security measure. It was just past noon and the miners with their lunch buckets—thick, rugged, hardworking men—sat eating or taking a quick nap in the aboveground sunshine. They watched Justice with dark eyes as he was guided past them.

Inside, Nathan Burbank looked up, shook his head, and beckoned Justice into his office. The guard handed Ruff his guns and went back to his post.

"Well?" Burbank said. "What are we going to do?"

"I'm going to stop this sabotage," Justice said.

"Other men have tried. Some of them are dead."

"I'll stop it."

"All right." Burbank reached for a cigar, rolled it around between his fingers, and then put it back. His eyes flickered. "What can I do to help you?" Burbank seemed a lot more friendly today, and he explained why. "The *boss* was out here yesterday looking for you. She was pretty upset. She said that you were her man all the way and that if I wanted to keep my job, I was to go along with whatever you suggested."

"The lady can get rather firm," Justice said dryly.

"You're telling me?"

Outside somewhere a steam whistle blew. Ruff looked blankly at the mine manager.

"The lunch hour's over. The second shift is going back down," he explained.

"Fine. I'd like to go with them."

"What are you going to do down there?" Burbank asked with surprise.

"I don't know. I don't know what I'm going to do, period. I just want to look around, familiarize myself with things. See where and how you were sabotaged last time.

111

By the way, what kind of guard system have you got, Burbank? Seems to me it would be awfully tough for a man to slip in here without being noticed."

"Damn near impossible, I'd say. We've got twice as many people on guard duty after dark. Still, the man, whoever he is, gets through. That's what leads me to think that it's the Ute. Indians got their ways of moving."

"Could be," Ruff said without comment. "Or it could be that it's someone the guards wouldn't challenge, wouldn't suspect."

"Such as?"

"Maybe the mine boss," Justice suggested.

"Yeah." Burbank was holding his anger back. "Look, I realize you're trying to do a job, but it's not me, Justice. You forget I was cooperating with Les Coyle."

"You didn't have much choice there—any more than you have now. Cooperating can mean a lot of different things. You're in a pretty good position to cover things up, aren't you, Burbank?"

"Yes," the mine manager said, "I am."

That was all. No complaints, no protestations. Burbank did have spine, Ruff decided. And in some corner of his mind he found himself hoping that it wasn't Burbank who was trying to destroy the Never-Never.

"I'll call someone up to show you the mine," Burbank said at length. He walked to the door and called out to one of his assistants, "Get Hank Ryker before he goes down the shaft." Then he turned to Justice to explain. "Ryker's the foreman. He knows what's what."

"And what kind of man is he?" Justice asked.

"Hell, I don't know. Make your own judgments. You ask a hell of a lot of questions, Justice. Are you sure you weren't a lawman once somewhere?"

Ruff grinned. "You think I'd want to make a living this way?"

There was a thump on the door and a big-shouldered, smiling man came through. "This is Ryker," Nathan Burbank said.

Ryker wore a faded blue shirt with the cuffs rolled up over a faded red underwear shirt. His hair was dark and curly, dropping across a broad forehead. In the back of his skull was a bald spot, which would mature in time. The eyes were blue, amused. The shoulders were heavy with muscle from a lifetime of work in the mines. He flashed a white smile from a grime-darkened face.

"This is Ruff Justice, Ryker. He's taking over security for a time."

"For how long?" Ryker asked.

"Until we've stopped the sabotage," Justice said with determination.

"You want me to help?" The foreman scratched his ear.

"Just take Justice down the shaft and show him around. He'll let you know if he wants anything."

"Sure thing, Mister Burbank. Justice, better leave that rifle. I'd leave the other too if I were you. A gun's of little use down in the Never-Never. For one thing, there's the ricochets. Why, a bullet might bounce around until it came right back up your own muzzle. Then there's the gas—we've been into a little of that down low. It's all right if you leave it be. It stinks, but it hugs the floor and don't bother us. A gunshot, though, might be like touching off a powder keg. Could blow up the hole," Ryker said. He was grinning, but he was dead serious. Ruff took his suggestion.

Outside the office it was clouding up again. "Rain . . . that's bad for us. We got men pumping Number Two right now, have been for a week, since we got flooded out on purpose by somebody. There's also faults in Number Two. A lot of water comes in. A man drowned there,"

Ryker said, his smile falling away briefly. "Someone killed him."

"How do you go about flooding a shaft on purpose?" Ruff asked.

"With Number Two it was easy. We were working hydraulics in her until it got too deep and she stopped draining. We had a monster holding tank up top." He lifted his chin to the mountain, where Ruff could see a wooden tank caulked with pitch.

"Ran hose from that, did you?" Ruff asked.

"Yeah, we did. Three of them, four-inchers. Number two showed a lot of soft material inside a hard shell. We washed her out as much as we could, then started blasting. Someone got in one night and opened up the tank again. Next morning she was flooded twenty feet deep on the third stope. Harry Watkins volunteered to go down and have a look. He never came back. Found him three days later when she drained."

"Wouldn't someone have to know a little about the Never-Never to even think of that trick?"

Ryker shrugged. "Everyone in town knows a little about the Never-Never. Miners talk. They talk at home and they talk in saloons. Someone just got a bright idea."

They had come to the head of the shaft. Above the entrance a crudely lettered sign said, NUMBER TWO. Justice looked at the vast, jagged mouth of the mine shaft and shook his head.

"Don't get nervous underground, do you, Mister Justice?"

"I do, but that won't stop me."

"Good." Ryker grinned. Inside, he got a lamp with a polished reflector behind the wick and two helmets, each with a small copper tank and a glass-shielded wick. "Newest thing. Carry a little coal oil around right on your head. Find one that fits. Here."

He handed Ruff the lantern and took another, and they started on down. Thirty feet down the line they found an ore cart sitting idle, a miner leaning against it.

"Get it on down, Mike," Hank Ryker said. "Lunch is over."

"Getting some air, Hank. The gas is heavy down below."

"You mean it's getting worse?" Ryker looked worried.

"Bad enough. If anyone was to ask me, I'd say that Number Two ought to be shut down for a while."

"I guess no one's going to ask," Hank replied. He slapped the man's shoulder. "Try again after you've got your wind." A little farther on Ryker said, "He might be right, but you noticed Mike was the only man up there— he's a complainer. Think I might have to let him go, though I hate to; he's got family."

The shaft had widened out and now there were lanterns along the stony corridor every forty feet or so. Twin steel rails ran at an ever-sharper angle into the maw of the shaft. A steel cable lay inert between the rails, the means by which the heavy ore carts were winched up by a crew above.

They reached a pit dropping straight into the heart of the earth. There three men were winching up iron buckets, which were dumped it into the carts.

Ruff was introduced. "He'll be in charge of security for a time. I'm showing him around. Ned? How about a ride in your bucket?"

"Sure," the miner answered. He had a protuberant brow over eyes hidden and blurred in shadow.

"There's a ladder, but it's a hell of a climb," Ryker told Justice, stepping into the iron bucket, which was ten feet in diameter and well-rusted. Ryker touched the rust with a finger. "It was underwater. This shaft's where most of the damage was done."

The winch creaked, the bucket jerked, and they started down into the deep dark shaft.

"How's the mine look, Ryker? Is there plenty of ore, good ore?"

"Mister, this is the richest thing I've ever seen or imagined. I could show you a place where you can spread your arms and not touch anything but pure gold. This ore you see coming up now isn't so rich; that's because we can't just work the vein. Pretty soon we'd have a wandering narrow shaft going straight down into hell. Besides, what you see is rich enough to make many a mine owner's mouth water."

Ruff nodded silently. He didn't much enjoy riding down in that bucket. It swung gently from side to side, their lanterns and helmet lamps playing eerily on the rough stone walls of the surrounding shaft.

"Sixty feet is all it is," Ryker said. "It seems like more because we go slow. You wouldn't want a faster drop, though."

They finally touched bottom and clambered out, hearing the sounds of hammers, seeing lights moving strangely in the distance. Once a voice, muffled and distant, came to them.

There was a lot of mud underfoot.

"From the flooding. We timbered up again, but still the men don't much like Number Two. They think it's a bad-luck shaft. Some of them have started seeing little spooks." Ryker laughed and shook his head. He didn't understand why Ruff wasn't laughing. But then, Justice knew. He knew about the underground spirits.

"I'll show you where we found the second body," Ryker said. "Down the right-hand shaft here. Bob Courtner was his name. His head was bashed in. Bob was running the pump up top after the flooding. For some reason he came down. Maybe he heard something, I don't know, it's—"

"Ryker," a miner, hands cupped to his mouth, called.

"Yeah?" Ryker turned.

"We got a problem with the shoring."

"Okay. Want to wait here, Justice?"

"I'll poke around a little. Go take care of your work."

"All right. Watch your step. There's a down shaft about forty feet up there. It would have been boarded up, but we haven't worked that for a long while; ore played out."

Ruff said he would be careful. Ryker strode away, his light vanishing around a bend, and Justice stood alone in the cold tunnel, not caring for it much. He could hear voices, see dim flashes of light from time to time, hear the creaking of machinery and of heavily loaded timbers.

He started on, looking up at the ceiling where a mountain rested on those timbers, then down at the floor where there were still twin grooves cut in the stone. There had been a pair of rails running up this shaft as well, until the vein petered out. He was working uphill now. The mud hadn't reached here yet. Ruff's lantern showed dark walls cut by streaks of pale quartz, and here and there even his inexperienced eyes caught the gleam of something shining dully, promising wealth and ease and power. Yes, there was still gold there.

The down shaft opened up suddenly before Ruff. He kicked a rock into it, and it seemed to fall for many, many seconds before striking bottom, the echo ringing back. He eased around the opening cautiously and went on, wondering about the man who had died here, wondering what the saboteur had been doing down here at all.

Whoever he was, he had tried flooding the place, failed, and then returned—but for what?

Justice's head suddenly began to hum with a notion.

Blood pulsed solidly through his temples. He *knew*. He knew, or thought he knew, why the vandal had returned to the Never-Never.

It had to be.

He cared about only one thing—destruction—and so there could be but a single reason for his return. The shaft had been booby-trapped.

Timbers cut? No, that was too time-consuming. The saboteur ran the risk of being trapped himself if he estimated wrong.

Something had been done. Something that the dead miner had discovered or threatened to discover. Something that had not worked because the decision had already been made not to work the right-hand shaft where the vein of ore had dwindled.

The lantern caught the silver thread, and Ruff's lip curled back savagely.

There it was. Gleaming faintly, slender, deadly. Justice looked right and left, but saw nothing. The wire ran across the shaft at boot level and disappeared at either end behind two upright timbers.

He stepped over the wire and held up his lantern.

The mechanism was behind the twelve-by-twelve upright. He didn't have to look very close to see what it was. The trip wire ran to the trigger of a cocked .44 revolver that was secured to the timber with three big cleats. In front of the revolver's muzzle was a bundle of dynamite, enough to blow up the entire shaft and bring the Never-Never down on itself. The only reason it hadn't worked was that no one had passed this way since the trap was set. It must have caused the maker of the device much confusion.

The bootstep was light on the gravel floor of the mine shaft, but loud enough to bring Ruff's head around. When he turned, he saw the man, iron bar upraised.

Justice flung himself to one side as the bar sliced air and missed his skull by inches, ringing off the stone.

"Stop it, you fool," Justice shouted. "There's a bomb . . ."

But the man with the iron bar wasn't listening. He swung viciously at Justice, who wasn't able to roll away fast enough this time. The iron bar struck shoulder bone, and his body shrieked with pain.

His shoulder was numb as he staggered to his feet and backed up against the wall of the tunnel. Ruff's right hand was working, however, and from the sheath the big bowie emerged, its blade gleaming, razor-edged, ready.

Ruff looked at his feet in horror. They were inches from the trip wire, and the man with the iron bar, moving in, seemed unaware of it.

"Stop, you damned fool. You'll blow us up. Us and the mine and everyone in it!"

If the man believed him, it didn't stop him. He swung the iron bar again, but Justice ducked, moved in, and cut upward with the big bowie. He caught flesh and bowels, and the man who had wanted to kill screamed like a woman, screamed and pawed at the knife and dropped his iron bar.

The man started to fall back, and Ruff couldn't catch him with his numb arm. He couldn't catch him, and just behind the dying man was the trip wire set to blow them all off the planet.

Ruff ground his teeth and closed his eyes. He couldn't hold the man up, and so they fell together. Justice hit the ground hard and didn't move a muscle. Nothing had happened; they had missed the wire. Peering across the dead man's body, Ruff saw something that caused a cold sweat to break out on his face and chest. The dead man's hand was resting on the silver wire, drawing it down slightly. Justice was pinned beneath the body, his good arm and one leg caught there, immobilized.

He didn't trust his left arm much. When he tried to move it, the arm twitched clumsily, and he let it fall to his side, panting with tension.

Footsteps brought his head up. Running footsteps, approaching too fast.

"Stop!" Justice called out. "Hold up there!"

"Justice?" Ryker's voice shouted back. Then he was there, nearly on top of the wire, another miner with him.

"For God's sake, Ryker, stop!"

When they didn't, it was only inches from the wire. Ryker stared uncomprehendingly at Justice, who was tangled up with a corpse on the floor of his mine shaft.

"Who is it? What happened?"

"Never mind that for now. Christ's sake, Ryker, there's a trip wire in front of you. Look down. Shine that lamp." Then they saw the wire, and the other miner stepped back as if he had seen a rattler.

"What is it?"

"Connected to a bundle of dynamite, Ryker. The hand—the dead man's hand. Lift it off, please. Very carefully."

Ryker's eyes were wide as he crouched to do the job, but do it he did, carefully grasping the dead man's wrist and moving it aside.

"Now, what?"

"Now get me up. I don't mind killin' 'em, but I'm damned if I'm going to lie down with 'em."

They untangled Justice and got him to his feet. "Have you got any wire cutters handy?" he asked.

"Willie," Ryker said to the other miner, "get on back and find some cutters, quick."

Ruff, rubbing his shoulder, which was still fiery and half-numb, showed the mechanism to Ryker.

"Simple," the mine boss said.

"Yes, and it would have worked too."

"Who's this on the floor?" Ryker rolled the dead man over. "Jake Rollins?"

"One of your people, I take it."

"One of the better ones. Why would he try to destroy the mine?"

"It wasn't him," Justice said. "This man didn't know about the bomb. He wasn't the one who set it."

"Then, why?" Ryker began.

Justice showed him why Rollins had tried to kill him. The folded-up piece of paper in the miner's shirt pocket explained everything:

Ruff Justice, Five Hunert Bucks.

Ruff Justice had just met his first Longden bounty-hunter. He crumpled up the paper and tossed it away. Willie was back with the wire cutters, and they clipped the trip wire before disarming the bomb. There was nothing special about the Colt .44 that had been used, nothing remarkable about the dynamite.

"It came from our stores," Ryker admitted. "We've got plenty of this stuff up there. Almost anyone can get it, I suppose."

"But not everyone *would*," Justice said. He had feeling back in his shoulder, but all that meant was that it hurt like hell. At least it didn't seem to be broken. Ryker didn't get his meaning.

"I don't understand," the foreman said.

"What I mean is, *you* wouldn't have set this bomb. Not here. You know this shaft isn't used anymore. Nathan Burbank would know that, as would most of your crew, maybe all of them. Why set a bomb when you know it will never go off?"

"Then it was someone from the outside."

"I think so, yes. Unless my thinking is off somewhere. It can't be anyone who works for the mine."

"Then, who?"

Ruff Justice could only shrug. "I wish to hell I knew, because this man doesn't kill singly, by accident. This was meant to kill by the scores, anyone who happened to be around, everyone. This was done by a special kind of man, Ryker. It was done by a madman."

11

"Madman," Burbank said. "*You* are a madman, Ruff Justice."

"I expect. Nevertheless I'm going to do it. We haven't gotten anywhere any other way."

"But to spend the night alone in the Never-Never! It's sheer hazard. Besides, what makes you think this maniac will be there tonight?"

"I don't know if he will or not, but I do know he will be back—sometime. Sometime soon. He seems to be pushing things, to be in a rush for one reason or another. Look at how fast things have happened lately."

"If he does come," Ryker said, "what can you do anyway, except likely get yourself killed?"

The mine foreman had a point. Justice, who had been standing at Burbank's window watching the miners load themselves into wagons to be driven to Denver, home, or the hot spots, shrugged.

"I don't know. But he's good at getting onto the grounds. He must be watching everything that happens.

He can't see me underground, however; that's the place to be, then."

"I wouldn't spend the night down there myself," Ryker admitted. "True, day and night would seem to make no difference underground, but you're alone and . . ."

"And what?"

"Nothing. It's just that sometimes you feel as if there are others down there, others that don't belong."

"Dark spirits," Ruff said, and Ryker shot him an amazed glance.

"I don't know what you two are talking about," Burbank said. "All I know is that it's hazardous as hell. Anything can happen, even without a madman around. Gas explosion, cave-in, stepping down a shaft. With the madman . . . I don't like it."

"You don't have to," Ruff said.

"No." Burbank sighed, placed his hands flat on his desk, and rose. "Do what you want, then. It's your life. I'll tell Ned."

"Don't tell anybody anything," Ruff said sharply.

"I thought you had decided that it couldn't have been any mine employees, as the bomb was set on a disused shaft."

"That's what I *believe*. I don't want to risk my life on it, though. Also, would your security people, for instance, know that you had decided to give up working that seam? How about your mule skinners? No, I didn't think so."

"All right," Burbank grumbled. "Have it your way. You'll be completely alone."

"Then there won't be anyone at my back to worry about, will there?" Ruff Justice asked.

Burbank didn't have an answer. Ruff was provided with a coat and a lantern. He was given some food— bread and cheese, smoked venison—and a canteen full of water. Then everyone just went home. Every one but Justice, who stood for a time in the mouth of Number Two, watching the orange sunset, wondering who was crazier, himself or the madman who wanted to blow up the Never-Never.

When the sky was purple and gold and the shadows pooled in the long valleys into inky lakes, Justice went down into the mine.

He had studied the map of the mine in Burbank's office, but it was a maze of shafts, ventilators, and stopes. The mountain was a virtual honeycomb. The madman— when he came, if he came—could be anywhere; he could have anything at all on his mind. But Justice had his hearing. He wouldn't be able to see the man, not at first, but anything that moved inside the mine would be heard. Water dripping, a shelf of ore sloughing off, the whispery tread of a rat in a dank shaft.

And the footsteps of a killer.

Ruff settled in. Near the down shaft of Number Two he waited, eating his supper. There was a wooden bench beside the bucket winch where the miners who operated it rested. It would do for Justice.

It was cold, very cold. Everything was silent. Justice's own chewing seemed loud in his ears. It wasn't going to be much fun, but it needed to be done. Had to be.

"I haven't forgotten, Les. He won't get away. This may take a long time, a very long time, but I'll get him."

Maybe.

The night passed and Ruff began to doubt the wisdom of this scheme. Outside, the pale moon had begun to rise slowly, lightening the sky. Down in the depths of the earth it was eternal midnight. Small things scuttled here and there—rats or perhaps other dark, nameless things. Spirits offended by the digging up of their earth home.

Thinking that way made Justice wonder where

Tanglefoot was. Had the Ute decided to take a hand in this? Or had he, wisely, decided to go back into the mountains and leave the whites to their bloody confusion?

The small sound brought Ruff's head up as if it had been jerked by an invisible puppet master. His hand wrapped around the ax handle beside his wooden bench.

He listened a long while, waiting for a second sound, but none came. Nerves? He didn't think so. Ruff had been worried, scared, and desperate in his time, but he didn't have the sort of nerves that invent bogeymen and spooks.

The sound came again. It was distant. It was a tiny echo sound, like a bird in the far brush calling on a windy day. It also didn't belong in the Never-Never.

Ruff slipped out of his boots. The floor of the shaft was cold, but the boots, soft as they were, made too much noise. Simultaneously he placed his helmet aside. He couldn't use it or the lantern, not without alerting whoever, whatever it was.

He started down the shaft, moving by the dimmest of light, provided by the moon and by the still-fizzling wicks of the lamps along the walls.

Another sound, still indefinable, still distant. The ax handle in Ruff's hand was smooth and solid, reassuring.

He stepped around the corner of the shaft and came face to face with a huge man with a rifle in his hands. Justice swing a left to his oversized belly and slammed his right hand, the one with the ax handle, into the man's face. He went down, but not swiftly enough, not silently.

He groaned, and Ruff heard other voices.

"What was that?"

"Shut up, Ozzie."

"It was Bert, I think. Who the hell . . . ?"

"Give me that fuse and shut up. We're not being paid to gabble. Bert can take care of himself."

"Something happened to him, I tell you," the first man insisted.

"Then go and see, dammit! But first give me the fuse."

Ruff was crouched beside the unconscious man. He could see the flickering of a lantern, see a shadow cast on the wall of the cavern. He had the intruder's rifle, but he knew better than to fire it because of the gas, the possibility of an explosion that could bring the mountain down. But did *they* know?

Ruff's eyes flickered to the iron-ore cart standing empty, inert on the rails before him. Moving in a crouch, sock feet silent against the rock floor, he slipped behind the iron cart.

Farther down the corridor one of the men was moving toward him, coming cautiously up the shaft. Farther still, the other man worked. Justice slipped the brake on the iron cart and hung on behind, head low.

"Look out!" Ozzie shouted.

"What in Christ's . . . ! Get out of there, get out!"

Ozzie was too slow. The cart slammed into him and Ruff felt the thump as the heavy wheels crushed his body. The other one was pressed against the wall, eyes wide. Justice leapt from the back of the cart as it rumbled by and went rushing off into the depths of the Never-Never.

When the thug went for his gun, Ruff hit him with the ax handle. He hit him hard, hearing a solid, wooden sound as hickory met skull bone. The thug went down hard, and when Ruff went to check, he found no pulse. Ruff's mouth tightened slightly, his eyes narrowed with disgust.

He found the powder charge easily. They hadn't bothered to hide it. Fifty pounds of black powder with a slow fuse, maybe fifteen minutes' worth, ready to light. Justice yanked the fuse and went back to search the body. He found nothing but fifty dollars in gold.

They had been paid in advance, then. But who had paid them? Justice walked back up the tracks past the broken body of the man who had been run over by the ore cart.

The third man was gone!

Cursing, Justice sprinted toward the mouth of the cave, his bare feet flying. He stubbed a toe on an unseen chunk of ore and hobbled on. Reaching the mouth of the tunnel, he looked down at the dark mine yard. Nothing. Bert had made his escape good.

Maybe.

Justice got his boots and guns. He slipped down to the yard himself and was immediately stopped.

"Hold it there, mister." An armed guard came forward, rifle level.

"It's Justice, remember me?"

"Yeah." The guard was dubious. "What are you doing up here in the middle of the night?"

"Chasing the man who's been trying to wreck the mine. Let's find him."

"Which way was he heading?" the guard asked.

"No idea. Back to town, I'd guess. And if he was scared enough, it would be in a straight line."

"Let's go." The guard started jogging toward the front gate, and Justice was beside him. They found the gate guard on the ground, his head staved in.

"Damn, they've killed him."

"No," Ruff said, "he's alive. Watch the gate. I'm going to get my horse. When I get to town, I'll send the doctor out."

"Don't worry about that," the guard answered. "We'll

get Art into town somehow. You catch the bastard that did it, Mister Justice."

"I intend to. Believe me."

Because the man who did it was the key to many things. He had been paid by someone to blow up the Never-Never. He knew who had wanted that job done, and that was the same person who had killed Les Coyle. Ruff would find him, and when he did, he would talk.

The saddled bobtail was in the toolshed. Ruff swung aboard, slapped the sleepy buckskin, and rode hell for it, through the mine yard, out the gate, and into the moon-shadowed forest. Beyond, the lights of Denver gleamed dully like distant stars.

The other rider, Bert, wasn't far ahead of Justice. Dust from his passing still hung in the air, and as Ruff burst from the pines, he saw the dark rider on the flats ahead of him turn and then lean low across the withers of his horse, whipping it mercilessly.

Justice heeled the big buckskin roughly. He wanted this man, and the horse was of secondary importance. If the bobtail had to run all night, run until his legs were worn down to the knees, he would do it.

He didn't have to run that far, that long. In minutes they were into the city limits and the escaping rider was riding frantically up the still-busy streets. There was no dust here on the flats, only red mud, which flew from the dark horse's hooves, spattering passersby, turning heads, drawing raised fists and curses. Seconds later Ruff Justice, flagging the buckskin, raced past, drawing much the same response.

Miners scattered; ladies hoisted their skirts and made for the plankwalks. Justice noticed all of it only peripherally. His attention was on Bert, only on the escaping thug.

Bert wheeled his horse to the left, up a side street, and

Justice smiled grimly. He knew the street, knew it too well. He slowed the buckskin a little as he rode it up the raucous, lighted confines of Delaney Street.

The dark horse was lathered, its head hanging, reins free when Justice found it in front of Blue Boy Weaver's place.

Ruff swung down from the bobtail and stood in the street for a minute, watching the loafers on the porch. They were miners, with a scattering of cowhands. All of them looked tough; all of them were drinking or had been. Justice started up the porch.

"Where you going?"

The question came from a dark-bearded man with a flat nose. He was big and looked like he fancied himself.

"Inside," Ruff Justice said. He glanced around, seeing that they were beginning to crowd near him. He didn't like the feel of things a bit. Apparently Bert had a few friends—that, or Blue Boy had ordered Ruff kept out.

"Them buckskins you wear, don't see many around here."

"Not anymore," Justice agreed. He didn't want to delay much longer. The bully was getting up a head of steam, and the others had decided to help him push. "Now, if you'd let me pass, friend."

"I'm not your friend, tall man. What's your name, anyway? Ain't I heard of you?"

"Could be."

"Yeah, sure," the bearded man said, moving nearer yet so that Justice could smell the beer breath, the sour sweat. "Justice, ain't it? Aren't you some kind of wanted man, some kind of hard case?"

"Some kind," Justice said. He had the set-up pegged now. The man with the beard had been sent out to let the porch loafers know who Justice was, to let them know there was five hundred dollars on his head.

"Yeah." The big man rubbed his bearded chin. "Justice. Now, what was it I heard about a reward?"

Ruff didn't want to play out the hand. The man was trying to get him lynched. Besides, Bert might be out the back door by now on a fresh horse.

"I'm going in, please step aside," Justice said firmly.

He took a step forward, and the bearded man dropped a meaty hand on his shoulder. "Hold it, Justice! Boys, this here's the man Chase Longden—"

Ruff whirled around, slapped the man's hand away, and when the thug tried to grab him again, he cut loose with a sharp left hook that landed on the point of the black-bearded chin. The big man sat down hard on the plankwalk and stayed there.

"Excuse me," Justice said, and the others parted for him as he walked through the red door into Blue Boy Weaver's den.

Blue Boy himself was waiting. There wasn't any mistaking the man. He had made a living through extortion, threatening to break windows and arms and legs if he wasn't paid by the decent merchants for protection, and doing it—often. He was cruel and huge and skilled in brutality. Blue Boy had greasy, thin blond hair with a wave in front, tiny eyes framed in scar tissue, arms that bulged with muscle, straining the seams of the plaid jacket he wore. He had a gold-and-black-striped vest on, a heavy gold watch chain, and two ruby rings. There was a huge cigar in his teeth as he came forward, three armed men behind him.

"You," he said, "you ain't wanted here."

"Where's Bert?"

"Who?"

"Bert is his name. He works for you, I suppose, or you keep him around for odd jobs. He was out at the Never-Never with a man called Ozzie and another whose name

I didn't get, trying to blow up the mine. I want to talk to Bert, since the other two can't talk anymore."

"He's here," Blue Boy Weaver said surprisingly. He was up on the balls of his feet, smiling a broken-toothed smile. "You can see him, cowboy—just come through me and I'll let you do it."

"With those gunhands siding you?"

"They won't bother us any."

"That's right," the man in the doorway behind Justice said, "they won't bother you at all." And Jody Sharpe came in, scatter-gun in hand. "Ty's at my back, Blue Boy, so don't look for any help. You others shuck your guns. I heard most of what you said, Justice. It's all true?"

"All true, Jody."

"Go ahead, then; search the place."

"Wait a minute," Blue Boy Weaver bellowed. "I know the law. You ain't searching my place without a warrant."

"Then I'll get one," Jody snapped.

But by then it would be too late, and everyone knew it—that is if the crooked judge would even issue a warrant to search Blue Boy's place.

"We don't need a warrant, Jody," Ruff said quietly. "Blue Boy said he'd let me look."

"The hell I did! I said if you came *through me*, Justice!"

"Yeah." Ruff Justice was unbuckling his gun belt. "That's the deal. Get ready, Blue Boy, because I'm coming through you."

And Blue Boy Weaver smiled. He smiled with hungry joy. He lived to break bones and gouge eyes, and it had been a long while since he had gotten much fun out of life. He had others to do the hurting and killing now, but here was Justice offering himself up.

"All right," Blue Boy said, taking off his coat. "You got

132

the deal, cowboy. You come on, do your best, because old Blue Boy is going to tear your head right off and tuck it under your arm for you. And if you don't think I'm the man that can do it, then you are just a fool, boy."

Justice figured that Blue Boy was probably right. He *was* a fool. Blue Boy in shirt-sleeves looked twice as big as Blue Boy in a coat. When he rolled up his cuffs, thick forearms heavy with ropy muscle came into view. Blue Boy was still smiling.

"Come on, boy. Let's see the color of your blood."

12

Ruff Justice hung his belt gun on the chair beside him. There had been a piano playing when he had come in. Now it was silent. This was better entertainment. In the background Ruff saw some yellow-backed money change hands. Someone was crazy enough to bet on the scout. Justice wouldn't have minded putting a little down on the other side.

Ruff had fought men, and lots of them, but he couldn't recall facing a thing like Blue Boy Weaver before. A thing that enjoyed hurting and was skilled at it.

"Well?" Blue Boy said as Justice turned to face him.

There wasn't any way to put it off, so there was no sense hesitating. Justice put up his hands, and Blue Boy Weaver threw a high arcing overhanded punch. It hit nothing but forearm and shoulder, but Justice felt his body shake down to his toes.

It was his injured shoulder that Blue Boy had hit, and the old pain flared up briefly. Justice wasn't sure which blow had hurt more: the miner with his iron bar or Blue Boy Weaver with a bare fist.

Justice jabbed at Blue Boy's swollen face, punching his nose twice, faking another jab, hooking in a tenuous right. Blue Boy took the punches, scowling as each landed, but hardly backing up.

"I'm going to rip you apart, Justice," Blue Boy said savagely. "I ain't Chase Longden, though I bet I'm going to have some of Chase's gold money soon, earned with my bare hands."

Maybe so. Blue Boy waded in, hooking with either hand. Justice blocked a left to his ribs with his elbow, but the punch from the other side landed above the liver, flooding Ruff's side with exquisite pain.

Anger flushed Ruff's face now, anger and determination. He backed into a round table, tossed it aside, and threw a right against Blue Boy's ear. That one was a good one, landing with authority. Blue Boy's head was jarred to one side and his left foot slipped. A purple worm of blood snuck down from his ear, through the long sideburn.

"You got some muscle, boy," Weaver snorted, "but not enough. I'm through toying with you."

Blue Boy grabbed a chair from behind him and winged it at Ruff's head. Justice managed to duck as the chair flew past, breaking glass somewhere behind him. Weaver kicked out with a booted foot, trying to crush Ruff Justice's knee.

Ruff brushed against another table and it went down. Hooking a left to the ribs and another over Blue Boy's guard, Ruff felt his feet slip in a pool of beer from the toppled table.

He went down hard, fear rising in his throat. That was where Blue Boy, the old stomper, would want Justice: on the floor, where he could go after the kidneys, the groin, the face with his boots while Justice lay helpless.

He came in, all right, crying out with savage joy. Ruff

rolled, grabbed Blue Boy's foot, and came up; the big man went to the floor himself, his head thudding against the planks.

Justice regained his balance and waited as Weaver rose, looking red-eye angry now. His good suit had the knee torn out and beer soaked the leg. Several men laughed as Blue Boy slipped while trying to rise. Weaver couldn't take that. He was to be feared, not mocked. Sloshing around in a pool of beer wasn't what he had in mind.

"Get ready, boy. I'll show you some tricks you never seen before."

But Ruff had seen a few, and when Blue Boy came in trying to stamp down on his foot with his boot heel, Justice gave the big man a forearm across his throat instead, and Blue Boy, choking and cursing, backed up hastily.

Weaver was far from finished. He had bitten the tip of his tongue off and now his mouth was bleeding as well, but he had been hurt before, much worse, and it was only a part of the game.

The way you won the game was by hurting the other man more. And that was just what Weaver meant to do.

He came in again, his oxlike shoulders winging rights and lefts at Justice's head. One of them got through Ruff's upraised forearms, and it landed hard on the jaw hinge. Ruff was staggered, and he felt the buzzing begin in his head. He moved back, taking a barrage of blows on his forearms, elbows, and shoulders as he ducked and bobbed, trying to avoid the haymaker Blue Boy Weaver was trying to land.

Ruff was moving back, giving way before the trip-hammer blows. He could hear the cheering of the crowd like the roar of a distant train. The wagonwheel chandeliers overhead spun in dizzy circles. Ruff's back came up against the solid oak of the bar, and there was no more backing up. He set himself and fought back with desperate strength.

Justice uppercut to get a little breathing room. Blue Boy's head snapped back, but it didn't seem to hurt him much. Ruff kicked at Blue Boy's midsection with his right foot, and Weaver knocked it aside, boring in again, thumping at Ruff with those heavy punches.

Justice ducked away, forearms over his face. The last right hand shot from Weaver's arsenal had hurt, hurt bad. But Justice wasn't about to let Blue Boy know that. He laughed out loud, throwing his hair back.

"Is that all you've got, Weaver? What the hell are the people in this town so scared of? Looks to me like your reputation's gone to flab."

Weaver roared with anger and he came forward again. He hooked a right to Ruff's head and then grabbed Justice, yanking him toward him.

Blue Boy was going for the eyes. An old-time gouger, he still habitually wore his thumbnails long and filed to a point. Justice jerked his head to one side frantically, feeling a thumbnail rake across his cheek, drawing blood.

Justice slammed an ineffective knee at Blue Boy's groin then; failing there, he bashed his forehead against the big man's nose. Blood gushed over both men as Weaver fell back with a howl of pain.

It wasn't the first time that nose had been broken, however, and Blue Boy wiped away the blood angrily, coming in again, throwing chairs aside as Justice, panting, stood waiting.

Ruff had his wind and his balance again. He jabbed at Blue Boy's face, trying to damage the nose further. Blue Boy swatted away three punches in a row, but the fourth found its bloody mark.

The crowd seemed quieter now. Expecting Blue Boy to finish Justice quickly, they had worked themselves up to a peak of excitement early. Now, as Justice lasted, they fell silent, watching with the same interest, but with doubt creeping into their minds.

There was some in Blue Boy's mind now too. Justice could see it in his eyes. Blood coated the big man's face. The eyes were slightly dull, and his breathing was uneven, labored through his broken nose.

But he wasn't going to stop. Blue Boy Weaver wasn't made that way. He had never been beaten and he wouldn't be now—he refused to be. If he let this narrow scout beat him, he might as well move out of Delaney Street, out of Denver. He'd never hear the end of it.

Blue Boy advanced again. He missed with an overhand right, a wild windmilling punch, and then missed with a left as Justice ducked away. Blue Boy grunted with the effort of each punch now. He just didn't have the wind for a long fight. He had been a one-punch fighter, a gouger and stomper all his life. He had always made sure he got his man early.

This was just a little too much. Frustrated, Blue Boy winged another chair at Justice. It missed and smashed the long bar mirror behind Ruff.

Blue Boy, with a sound almost like a grunt of despair, moved in again. He had Justice against the bar again and he was determined to take him now, but Ruff ducked away.

Ruff stabbed a left into Blue Boy's face three times, and each time Blue Boy winced. Tears ran from his pale eyes. Roaring, Blue Boy came in, ignoring the pain, and Justice's stunning right hand landed below his ear and staggered the big man again. Blue Boy careened into the bar and reached for the whiskey keg mounted there. Ripping it from its moorings, he heaved it at Justice. The keg, which must have weighed a hundred and twenty pounds, flew past Justice and exploded, spraying Blue

Boy's rotten hooch everywhere. Someone in the crowd moaned a protest.

But Blue Boy came in again.

His shirt was in rags, his grizzly-bear arms were held too low. His face was a mask of blood. His eyes showed some cloudiness. Ruff had him. He knew he had him, but he needed to be cautious about it. You don't play games with a man like Blue Boy Weaver. You chip away at him, chip away—and meanwhile Bert was possibly making his getaway.

Blue Boy pawed at Ruff now rather than snapping punches at him. When he tried to grab Ruff's shirt front, he missed by six inches. Justice jabbed and winged in an occasional right-hand shot, testing. Just testing.

Weaver couldn't stand to be beaten, but there was defeat in his eyes, defeat and despair. He gave it one more try. He rumbled in, using both hands to punch, neglecting defense entirely. He wanted to smash Justice, to pulverize him.

He should have used a little more defense.

Ruff saw the opening, and he let it go without hesitation—a sharp, short right hook that landed on the shelf of the jaw, and Blue Boy Weaver went down face forward into the pool of whiskey in which playing cards floated like tiny colorful rafts. He never got up.

Justice turned and walked to his guns. He hoped the wobble in his knees wasn't too noticeable. Weaver was all sorts of evil things, but he could hit. He could hit like a mule.

"Ready?" Justice asked Jody Sharpe. The deputy was still watching the crowd, gun ready, but no one seemed interested in interfering now.

"Yeah. You all heard Weaver—he told Justice we could search the place if we went through him. I think Justice has done that. Why don't you boys do yourselves a favor—go across the street to Longden's, or go home. There's not going to be anything else happening here tonight."

They more or less took his advice. There was some money changing hands, a few curses, grabbing of hats or poker winnings, and then they were gone. Ruff never saw the last man get prodded out by Sharpe. He was already working his way systematically through the place, trying the storeroom first.

He entered cautiously, pistol held in a battered, stiffening hand. The room was dark, smelling of sawdust and green beer and tar. Ruff worked his way through the barrels, looking behind them, among the crates. There was nothing there. When he emerged, Sharpe joined him.

"I looked in Blue Boy's office," Sharpe said. "Nothing there but an opium cake and a pipe. Enough to hold Blue Boy for a time, I'd guess. Ty's upstairs looking, but I think Bert got out the back."

"Looks like it," Ruff said gloomily.

Ty stuck his head over the rail above them. "Empty, Jody. No one here but one of those Chinese girls, and she ain't really here. She's in lotus land somewhere."

"All right. Forget the girl. Come on down, tie Blue Boy up, and march him over to the office."

Justice had opened the back door of Blue Boy's saloon. By a struck match he could see the footprints in the mud. Very fresh, likely but not positively Bert's. A horse had been waiting and now that horse was gone. Justice looked to the dark skies and shook his head.

"What's the matter, Justice?"

"The whole damn mess. I've never done so much moving around to accomplish so little."

"We got Blue Boy."

"I don't care if he gets a hundred years for selling opium and Chinese leg, frankly. I want the man who

140

killed Les Coyle. That is what I want. And I'm not a step closer to him."

"Maybe, maybe not. Maybe it was Blue Boy that did it, Justice. Maybe we can get him to talk. Ty's pretty good at that."

"Jody!" Ty cried at the front door of the saloon. He had a Chinese boy with him, and both looked excited. Ruff and Jody looked at each other and hurried that way.

"What is it?" Justice asked. "Bert . . . ?"

"It ain't Bert, Justice. It's the Duchess. It's Katie Price, someone's shot her."

Ruff stood immobilized for a moment, then he was sprinting toward the door, toward the bobtailed buckskin. Jody Sharpe called something after him, wanting Ruff to stop, perhaps, but Justice never heard him.

He hit the saddle of that buckskin and was riding hell for it up Delaney Street before his butt touched leather. He was cursing out loud, a long-haired, battered demon racing up the muddy Denver street.

"Damn you, Justice. Stupid! Stupid!"

He had let her get shot, let Katie Price get it. It had made sense that the killer would try for Katie in the end. He had done everything else he could do to wreck the Never-Never without success. So why not kill the mine's owner? What better way to strike at the outfit than to go for its head?

"Stupid," Justice said again, grinding his teeth.

He had even suspected Katie, practically accusing her to her face. When he should have had someone watching her or been watching her himself, he was out rolling around in a mine shaft with some clumsy hireling.

The house loomed up, dark and square atop the hill where it sat brooding. Justice hightailed it up the driveway and swung down. There was a horse there, tied to the rail. The doctor, Justice guessed.

It was. The man sat with a drink of brandy in his hand just inside the door. He looked small and weary, his hands very white.

"This is getting to be a sad house to visit, Justice," the doctor said, "very sad."

"Why aren't you with her? Is she . . . ?"

"I'm not with her because I can't do anything else," the doctor flared up. He rubbed his head and sighed. "No, she's not dead. But she's shot up pretty good. A forty-four slug in her back. It passed through at an angle, taking a little lung tissue with it."

"How's it look?"

"It looks ugly, damned ugly," the doctor said, drinking his brandy. "I did my best. If you mean what sort of prognosis is there, I can't say. You've been a fighting man, I'd guess. You know how it is with gunshot wounds, especially those that affect the internal organs. If the infection stays down, she'll be all right. I think."

It wasn't very cheering news. "Can I see her?"

"If you want. You might not get much sense out of her. I used ether and she had several large jolts of brandy before that. She was rather incoherent when I saw her last."

Ruff looked across the cold, empty room. "Where the hell is everybody? She's got half a dozen servants, where are they?"

"One of the maids is acting as nurse—the little one, Consuelo. I armed two servants and put them out standing sentry."

"And where in hell's Harlon Staggs?"

"I couldn't tell you."

"Lily Sly? She was staying here."

"I don't know, Justice. The maid sent a boy to get me. I came and did my best. I don't know where anyone is. I don't know if Katie Price is going to make it. I don't know

142

what good any of this is. I don't know why I patch people together so they can die anyway, and I don't know why I drink so much."

The doctor rose unsteadily, picked up his hat and the bag it was resting on, and with a curt nod, went out, weaving slightly.

Ruff Justice was left alone in the empty, violent house.

13

Katie Price looked frail and helpless, lying in the big powder-blue bed, wearing a pale-yellow gown. It was as if the bullet had ripped her amazing vigor, her zest, from her, and this was all that was left, a small husklike thing that only resembled a woman.

The little nurse sat in the corner knitting, and Ruff flagged a thumb at her. She left the room, closing the door softly, and Justice pulled up a carved, gilt, velvet-cushioned chair to sit on beside the bed.

He sat bent forward, looking at her for a long while. Her lashes were long and dark and fine. Her eyelids were pale, veined with blue. Her eyebrows, normally arched in amusement, were flat and even. Her forehead was smooth and chalky, her lips too pale.

The eyes flickered open.

"What in hell happened to you, Justice?" she asked with a heavy, drugged drawl. "You're all beat up, mister."

"Blue Boy."

"Really?" She tittered a little. Doc was right—she was floating on ether and alcohol. "Sock him one for me?"

"Yes, I did, Katie, how are you?"

"Hurt." Her head rolled away and then back; her eyes, too glassy and bright, searched Ruff's face. She smiled and reached out weakly to touch his jaw. "Do you hurt, Justice?"

"Not bad. Katie, where's Lily?"

"Left. This morning. Took a buggy . . ." Katie yawned and drifted away.

"Katie, where did she go, and where's Harlon Staggs?"

"Went to get her things. I sent Staggs along with her. Woman can't carry trunks and all. It isn't right."

"Stay awake a minute longer, Katie, please! Who shot you?"

"Dunno . . ." she muttered.

"Katie, please . . ."

"Kiss me, Justice," she said, and the faintest smile curved her mouth.

"Listen, it's important, Katie. Tell me about it. What happened?"

"Shot me . . . give me a kiss, Justice, then let me sleep. A kiss for the Duchess."

Ruff slowly bent his head and kissed her. Her lips were papery, almost lifeless. When he drew away, she was smiling slightly, asleep.

Outside, Jody Sharpe waited.

"Did you know about this?" Sharpe demanded. He handed the wanted poster to Ruff Justice, who read it, scowling.

The poster was of Harlon Staggs, and he was wanted for murder. Kansas wanted him dead or alive. Ruff shook his head and handed it back.

"I don't know anything about his background except

that he worked as a bouncer at the old Scottish Wheel," Justice said. "How'd this come up?"

"It was tacked to my office door when Ty and I got back with Blue Boy Weaver."

"No idea who put it there?"

"No. Probably Staggs has made a lot of friends during his career."

"Likely."

"Do you know where he is, Justice?"

Ruff hesitated. "I've been more concerned with Katie Price."

"Does she know?"

"She's out cold, Jody. Doc gave her ether."

"Did she talk to you?" the deputy asked, folding the wanted poster carefully and putting it away.

"Not long. She wasn't making much sense."

"About the shooting, I mean. Did she tell you who shot her?"

"No. I don't think she knew."

"Harlon Staggs?" The deputy's eyes narrowed.

Ruff Justice shook his head. "I don't know. Why would he?"

"He's killed before. Maybe she found out. Maybe he wanted to lift some jewelry and cash and get down the road, and she found him."

"In that case she would have known who did it."

Ruff was only using a part of his mind. The other was more worried about Staggs than he would let Jody Sharpe know. Staggs might not have done the shooting here, but then again he might have. Right now he was up in Colson Canyon with Lily Sly—or supposed to be—and Justice was worried for the woman. Why he didn't want to tell Jody Sharpe what he knew, he couldn't say exactly. Maybe it was fear, fear that Harlon Staggs was the one who had killed Les Coyle and that someone besides

Ruff Justice would be there to put a bullet in him when they caught up with Staggs.

"How is the woman?" the deputy asked.

"I wondered if you'd get around to asking," Justice said.

"Hell, Justice," Sharpe said, scratching his head, "I don't think there's any need to get testy. There's been a hell of a lot going on around here. I'm trying to go a job that maybe don't fit me as well as it did Les Coyle."

"Sorry. Maybe Blue Boy knocked some of the manners out of me, Jody. Maybe I ought to get up to the hotel and get some rest."

Sharpe frowned. "I thought you were staying here?"

"No. I just left some of my gear here."

"Justice . . . Oh, hell, I guess you wouldn't tell me anyway," the deputy complained.

"No." Justice grinned. "I guess I wouldn't."

Sharpe was watching, hands on hips, when Justice went out, stuck a boot toe into the stirrup leather, and swung aboard the buckskin. Ruff lifted a hand, heeled the bobtail, and scatted.

It was dark, but the rising three-quarter moon was bright in the sky, lighting the trail toward Colson Canyon, toward the little cottage with the yellow curtains, where a killer had taken a young woman.

Staggs had been gone a long while with Lily, a hell of a long time if they had gone out that morning just to load a few of Lily's belongings onto a wagon to bring back to the house.

Lily had given it up, it seemed. Given up living alone, living with memories in that empty canyon. That was for the best, but now she had another tragedy to deal with.

"She'll be all right, Katie will be all right," Ruff said as his thoughts returned to the Duchess of Denver. He repeated it several times like magic words used to keep the bad things away. If you thought it, it was true, wasn't it? You couldn't lose faith.

The buckskin dipped down through a wooded hollow, and then the river was there, flowing into the long canyon as the moon silvered the dark grass below. He urged the weary buckskin on, willing it to a speed it just didn't have. The horse was game and it would run all night for him, but it just couldn't go any faster, and Justice found himself leaning far forward across the withers as if that would help, eyes straining for a first glimpse of the cottage.

It was in front of him suddenly—small, square, and there was a light on inside. Justice swatted the buckskin with his reins, and the gutsy little bobtail ran across the dark grass.

Above, the peaks seemed to crowd in on the little valley, gathering around to peer down at the house. The moon had grown smaller, whiter. There was a wagon in front of the house. Ruff felt his heart constrict. His Colt was in his hand without his recalling having drawn it. The buckskin was laboring, but Justice forced it to race on.

He swung down while the horse was still moving, and he sprinted for the house, shouldering through, gun ready, body coiled.

He spotted Staggs first.

Harlon Staggs was on the floor of the cabin, his head bathed in blood, and he looked up at Justice with pleading eyes.

Scowling, Ruffin went to the man, feeling cold inside, feeling a sickness growing. Dirty, it was a dirty game he had been dealt cards in.

"Help me up, Justice . . ."

"Think you can make it?"

"I'll try . . . Don't want to be down here. Cold."

Justice holstered his gun and crouched down. There was a bloody poker on the floor beside Harlon, lying where Justice had slept and played with a young, warm blond woman, a lonely, grieving widow.

"She did it?" Ruff asked.

"That's right. Lily Sly. Thought it was funny . . ." Harlon was lifted to his feet, shuddering with pain, and Justice placed him in the rocker.

"What was funny?"

"The Duchess told me to come along and help Lily load her stuff. Lily didn't want any part of it. Said she'd do it herself. The Duchess told her, 'You take Staggs. You can't be moving all that heavy property. Besides, Harlon needs some exercise.' "

Harlon laughed, but he winced with pain as he did so. Justice looked at the crease in Staggs' skull. "I know where some carbolic is."

"Got something for the beehive inside my brain?"

"Afraid not." Justice went to the kitchen and found the basin, sponge, and cloths where Lily had left them. Had that rap Justice had taken on the head given her the idea? Could be—she had that kind of mind. "Go ahead, Harlon."

"Not much to tell after that. We got here maybe nine this morning. I came in the house, and she asked me to have a look for some bauble she dropped, and when I bent over, she hit me with that poker. I woke up maybe an hour ago, but I couldn't get up. Dark, is it?"

"Yeah, it's dark now. Hold still. This is going to burn."

"Yeah." Staggs ground his teeth as Justice did what he could for the head wound. The skull didn't seem to be fractured, but why it wasn't, Ruff couldn't guess.

"You don't know where she is, do you, Staggs? Did she give you any hints?"

"No. She didn't say a word to me all the way out. I figured, well, she's thinking about the marshal, so I didn't try to pry any conversation out of her. She just bashed me and took off. I don't know where."

"The first place she went was back to Denver to put a slug in Katie Price's back," Ruff told him.

"Oh, Christ, no!"

"She's all right," Justice assured Staggs, although Ruff wasn't all that confident.

"Why? Lily Sly? Why, Justice?"

"She's mad, Staggs. Mad but clever, very clever. Why kill Katie Price? Why *not* kill her? Do you happen to know who the Duchess's nearest relative is?"

"Why, no, I . . . Jesus, it's Lily Sly, her cousin!"

"That's right. Who inherits the Never-Never, do you think, if anything happens to Katie?"

"I never thought of that. But what about all the rest of it? Damn, she must have—"

"She must have killed Les Coyle. Les was onto something. Maybe he had evidence in his hands without realizing it. Maybe as the time for their marriage got closer she resented him more."

"Resented him, for what?"

"For this." Ruff looked around the cozy little house. Staggs wagged his head.

"I don't get you."

"She hated this house. She told me that, but it didn't sink in. She hated living out here, the idea of living here forever, struggling, while her cousin lived in luxury. She told me all of that, Harlon, but you know how it is when you hear something without listening—it didn't sink in."

"You're sure?"

"Reasonably. Whoever killed Les was a guest at the party. A guest or one of the help. Someone who knew Les was changing his costume. Not many knew that. Lily would have."

"I don't understand this, Justice. If she hadn't tried to bash my skull in, I'd say you were crazy."

"Yes, I know."

"Why go about it the way she did, sabotaging the mine and all? Pure spite?"

"Some of it. She had to enjoy wrecking the Never-Never. But mainly it was to set up a smokescreen for something that was to come later—Katie's murder."

"Do I follow you?" Staggs asked. He was still obviously a little woozy.

"It's like this. She created a situation with a mystery saboteur. He could be anyone—the Ute, for instance. Someone who was trying to destroy the mine. People are hurt, bombs planted, shafts flooded. When Katie is killed, then they blame it on the saboteur and don't look for a motive like they usually do, starting with who inherits."

"The marshal wouldn't have looked closely at her anyway."

"A good reason for playing up to Les."

"Justice, I can't believe any woman is that cold-blooded."

"Touch your head here. There's a knot of evidence up there," Justice said. "That's what I think happened. Then, when she had her mind made up to kill Katie, she moved back to town. She wanted to sneak off today and then circle back. You got shoved off on her. It must have made her furious."

"So she bashed me."

"She had to, to get you out of the way. You were probably the one who was to take the blame for Katie's murder. She had dug up an old wanted poster on you and planned to give it to the deputy."

"Damm it, how do you know that?"

"Because she did just that. After she bashed you on the

head, she figured you for dead. Now she has to explain what happened to you. I figure she was inventing a new story on the way out here. That explains her silence, if you like—planning your murder and her alibi. All she would have to say was that you tried to attack her. Can you see a jury not believing that angel?"

Staggs just shook his head, because it fit, it fit only too well. "I guess I'd better get out of here, but I don't want to. I want to stay and see the woman hang if she shot Katie. Katie was the only one who tried to help me when I was in deep trouble. Katie knew about that murder charge, Justice, and she knew it was a frame. A man named Ken Hodges tried to gun me from behind. He shot me, and I turned with that bullet in my back and shot him dead. Hodges had more friends in Kansas City than I did, and the story got bent around."

"Sorry."

"Yeah, well, that's the way it goes. You say Jody's seen the warrant?"

"Yes, he has it."

"Damn. I want to see Katie. I need to know she's all right."

"You can't risk it, Harlon. You'll hang."

"I know it. I've got to skedaddle—if I can stay on a horse. Justice, you'll let me know, won't you?"

"I won't have to. The Duchess is news. It'll be in the Denver papers if . . . when she recovers. And it'll be in the papers if they hang Lily Sly."

"Will they? Would they hang the woman, Justice?"

"If I have anything to say about it, they will," Ruff Justice answered harshly. "I started out to get the one responsible for killing Les Coyle, don't forget. All right, I've nearly got her, and by God, she'll pay, Staggs. She's playing a man's game, she'll pay a man's price."

It was a question now of finding Lily so that she could

pay. Where would she go? Ruff spoke the question aloud.

"Not back after Katie?" Staggs said, coming half out of his chair with excitement. The big ugly man really cared for the Duchess of Denver.

"No. As far as Lily knows, she's dead. The house is well-guarded now anyway."

"Then she's hightailed it out of Denver."

"Why?" Justice asked.

"Why, well, she . . ." Staggs thrust out his lower lip in comprehension, nodding his head. "That's right, she don't know anything's gone wrong yet."

"As far as she knows, you're out of the way and Katie's dead. Lily Sly wouldn't try to get away, Staggs."

"Where, then?"

"The only place she could go, the only place she would feel she had unfinished work."

"The Never-Never? But why? You said this was all a scheme to remove Katie, to get hold of her money."

"That's right," Justice replied. "But then Katie has plenty of money. I believe she mentioned a number like twenty million dollars to me. Whether the Never-Never is destroyed or not, Lily thinks she will still be a rich woman."

"But there's no point in it, Justice!"

"I think she's obsessed with it. The Never-Never that made Katie rich and left Lily poor, that brought Katie a titled husband and left her with a poor lawman, that put Katie in the limelight, crowned her Duchess of Denver, and left Lily in the shadows."

"But to destroy it! Knowing there's more wealth there, knowing that men need to work there, knowing that someone is liable to get killed . . . Justice, that's plain mad!"

Justice nodded, his face grim, eyes cold. "I know it, Staggs. That's just what it is—madness."

They heard the pounding of horses' hooves, and the two men looked at each other, Staggs rising from his chair, his eyes narrowing with pain. He was unsteady on his feet, but he moved to the curtained window and stood beside Ruff, who had blown the lamp out and was now peering out at the night, at the riders.

"Come on out," a voice called. "We know you're in there, Justice, come on out and die."

14

Staggs had his pistol in hand, and he was leaning against the wall for support. His head wasn't feeling right, and it might not for a long while.

"Who the hell is it?" Staggs asked.

"Bounty-hunters," Justice answered.

"What? After me?"

"No, they don't know you're here. It's me they want. Chase Longden put a price on me."

"Justice!" a voice called from outside. "Come on out!" A pistol shot crashed loudly. The bullet ripped through the window frame, scattering splinters and shards of glass, burying itself in the opposite wall.

"Justice!"

"Who's out there?" Ruff called back. There was no point in pretending he wasn't in there.

"You never mind, just come out and take it."

There wasn't any disguising of the voice. Ruff knew Blue Boy Weaver when he heard him.

"You need the money that bad, do you, Blue Boy?" Ruff taunted.

"No, we've got another score."

"You couldn't do it with your fists. What makes you think you can do it with guns?"

A second shot flew through the window. Justice ducked low and Staggs pressed back against the wall. Ruff had been doing more than talking—he had been looking out the window, counting. The moon was bright and he could see the figures on horseback well enough. Staggs looked a question at Ruff Justice, and Ruff held up four fingers. Then, inclining his head, Ruff pointed toward the back door, and Staggs slipped off that way, gun in hand.

Ruff returned his attention to the front of the house.

"You coming out, Justice, or do we have to burn the place down?" Blue Boy yelled.

"How'd you get out of jail, Blue Boy?"

"I've got friends, lots of friends, Justice."

"Judge Ellis?" Ruff was stalling, trying to give Staggs a minute to get set.

"None of your damn business. They can't keep me in a Denver jail. The deputy's more worried about keeping the Ute from being hung anyway."

"The Ute? Tanglefoot!"

"Yeah, they caught him sneaking around up at the Never-Never. The miners are going to lynch him tonight. There'll be one less Indian in this country by midnight."

Ruff felt his heart contract, felt crimson anger begin to grow in his chest. A thug like Blue Boy Weaver could get out on bail within an hour of being arrested for selling opium or for using it to recruit Chinese prostitutes. Tanglefoot, watching the mine for Ruff Justice or trying to contact Ruff, had been convicted by popular prejudice and was going to be lynched on the sheerest circumstantial evidence.

Unless Ruff could get out of the house and into Denver . . . Just then it didn't seem real likely.

"Enough jawing, Justice. Are you going to come out and fight even up, or do we set the place on fire?"

"Even up?" Justice called back. "Does that mean just you and me? A fair fight?"

"Why, sure, Justice. A fair fight. You and me. Just like before."

If Blue Boy was trying to keep the sneer out of his voice, he wasn't having much luck at it. Even if Blue Boy had been sincere, the other men out there would have opened up on Ruff the minute he stepped out the door. They had come to kill, to make a handful of gold dollars. They wouldn't be denied that when a squeeze of the trigger could provide it.

Ruff glanced toward the back of the cottage, but it was too dark to see Staggs. Blue Boy and his men were having a conference out there. They had gotten smarter and had dismounted and now stood behind their horses where a casual shot by Justice couldn't tag them.

They would play hell getting Ruff out of the house unless they were prepared to wait and starve him out. But fire was a different story. Blue Boy had mentioned it, and he certainly wasn't above using it. Ruff saw a match lit, saw a torch catch fire. Rags soaked in coal oil had been wrapped around the sticks they carried.

Ruff didn't want to wait any longer. He fired three shots into the crowd of thugs and they scattered, a horse whickering in pain, one man shouting a curse. Ruff trailed Blue Boy with his sight, but the big man was only a dark mass against a black background as he merged with the trees beyond the toolshed, and Justice never squeezed off his shot.

A torch lay sputtering against the grass, but others were being lit in the trees. Ruff sighted on one, placing the front bead on the orange glow, and he triggered off. The torch fell and a man screamed with agony.

Blue Boy withdrew quickly. The night became silent, the yard empty. Ruff hadn't seen or heard Staggs since his first shot. Maybe that rap on the head had put him down again.

Ruff peered out the window, staring until his eyes were aching, until they were dry and his vision blurred. Where the hell had he gone? Blue Boy would be back, but where was he?

The answer was so obvious that Ruff could have kicked himself for not reacting better. He began to smell smoke and a little later to hear the crackling and popping of flame.

Blue Boy had given up on the front of the house and had come up on the sides where there were no windows. The fire had taken and was roaring up there, snarling and clawing at the roof with scarlet and gold talons. The smoke began to build inside the house.

Ruff was driven back by a sudden flurry of bullets aimed at the window. One was so near that it clipped the shoulder of his buckskin shirt without drawing blood.

That was close enough, and Justice backed away.

The smoke was very thick now, curling through the house, and glancing up, Justice was nearly struck in the face by a falling, fiery brand. The roof opened up and Justice could see the moon beyond a cloud of black smoke.

A bounty-hunter was on the roof; Justice could hear his boots. He crouched and waited, and when the man's face appeared in the hole in the roof, Justice shot him with the big .44 Colt.

The gun boomed, and the bounty-hunter was missing most of his face as he rolled off the roof, dropping to his deserved fate. They had come to find death, and by God, they would find it!

Justice felt a sudden draft and wheeled toward the back of the house. The kitchen door stood open. Staggs had made a run for it. A bounty-hunter shoved his pistol around the door frame and traded shots with Justice. Ruff's bullet tagged wood and hinge and whined off into the night, driving the man back.

Behind Justice the roof caved in and the front room filled with flames. He was trapped now. There was only one way out, and Blue Boy knew it. The back door stood open like a mocking mouth, a gateway to hell. Ruff Justice stood choking on the heavy smoke for a minute longer, then, lifting his eyes to the window beside the door, he made his choice.

It wouldn't fool them much, but even a split second's indecision might help. Justice put his forearm across his face and went headfirst through the window, spraying glass everywhere as he did so. Bullets crashed near at hand before he could regain his balance. Rolling, Justice fired a snap shot that caught one of the bounty-hunters square in the chest, hurling him back like a mule's kick.

Behind Ruff the house was in flames, ahead of him all was in darkness, and suddenly Blue Boy Weaver, shotgun in hand, was standing there, facing Ruff, who was still on his knees. There wasn't time, there just wasn't, Ruff thought.

"Blue Boy!" someone shouted, and the big man turned that way.

The guns scored the night with sound and flame, and Blue Boy Weaver dropped dead, a bullet through his neck, from side to side, destroying arteries and nerves, severing his spine so that his big head rolled on his limp neck for a second before he fell over lifelessly to the cold, dark earth.

Harlon Staggs was leaning against a tree, looking depleted, smug. "Got the bastard, didn't I?"

"You got him, Harlon." Ruff was on his feet walking toward Staggs. Blue Boy's shotgun still curled smoke. Staggs' chest and arm were a bloody mess. "Take it easy now."

"Yeah, sure. It's a little too late, Justice." He looked briefly toward the fountain of flame and smoke engulfing the little house. "Hell, I'm done," Staggs said. "I guess I saved 'em a hangin'. Take care of Katie, Justice, will you?"

"Sure, Harlon," Ruff promised, and then he watched the man fall over onto his face and lie there breathing roughly, blood staining the earth beneath him. Justice stayed with him the last few minutes, and when Staggs was gone, he watched as the entire roof of the house went down and all that Les Coyle had built was destroyed.

He found the buckskin not far from where he had left it, and he swung aboard the gutty little bobtail, pointing it toward Denver once more. They were going to try to hang an innocent man there tonight, if Blue Boy's report had been accurate, and Justice wasn't going to let them—if there was time, if the many-headed beast that a mob becomes hadn't already done the deed.

Justice didn't like mobs, he didn't like them at all. There was no reason in them, no restraint. They were made up of men who had gathered for only one reason: to do violence.

He rode on, weary, the moon chasing him toward town.

He could see the bonfires before he reached Bond Street. He could hear the sound, like the angry snarling of a subhuman thing. It was the mob talking, wanting to burn something, to smash windows and overturn wag-

160

ons. It wanted to be drunk and to stretch its stupid muscles. It never took much to get these beasts in motion. Sometimes they trampled themselves, turned on their own and on their leaders. The motives were different: sometimes they pretended they were celebrating good fortune. But that didn't make them any less deadly. Mostly they had a purpose for gathering, some noble cause, like seeing justice done, justice that degenerated at the drop of a hat into simple, mindless violence.

Ruff emerged from Delaney Street and onto Bond. The bonfires were at both ends of the street, flaring up hotly against the sky like reflections of the distant fire Ruff had seen. The crowd was shouting, grumbling, drunk and noisy, shifting and standing motionless before some sudden spur drove them to run here or there, tearing up plankwalk or breaking up a buggy to add to the fires.

In the middle of the street they had built a scaffold. A telegraph pole had been ripped up somewhere and dragged into the center of town. A hole had been dug, and the pole, fitted out with a noose, had been placed in it.

Justice walked his horse slowly up the street. They hardly noticed him. The marshal's office was locked up tight, some of the deputies undoubtedly barricaded inside. How long would they fight for Tanglefoot?

Everyone believed the Ute to be guilty of sabotaging the mine, of causing the accidents that took three lives. Ruff didn't think the deputy marshals were the kind to die for Tanglefoot's rights, although maybe he was wronging them.

There was only one way to the marshal's office and that was up the staircase, which ran from the store below to the landing above. The only way to get there was to go through the mob.

Ruff's lips tightened and he kneed the buckskin, walking it through the press of miners, most of whom carried clubs, ax handles, iron bars, a few guns.

"Hey, what the hell are you doing?"

"Watch out there, damn it!"

Ruff ignored them. The buckskin, nervous now, forced its way through the crowd. Ruff slipped his boots from the stirrups, and when he came abreast of the staircase, he reached up and swung over the rail and went on up.

He hammered on the door, and Jody Sharpe's voice called out, "Get away from that door before I blow you in half!"

"It's Justice, Sharpe."

There was a short silence. "What are you doing here?" Sharpe finally said.

"Let me in, it's important."

"You're out of this now, Justice. We've got your saboteur locked up in here."

"The hell you do," Ruff said in annoyance. "You're not even close. Tanglefoot didn't have anything to do with it."

"You know who did, I suppose."

"I'm getting tired of talking to a door, Sharpe."

"All right. Is the stairway clear?"

"For now." Ruff looked down to the street. They were still there, still swaying and growling, waiting for meat.

The door popped open and Justice was hustled inside. Ty Roosevelt and another deputy, a man in a striped shirt with scared eyes, looked around at him from out of the dim lantern light. They had guns in hand and boxes of gleaming brass cartridges on the office desk.

"You made a mistake coming here," Sharpe said.

"Did I? I didn't figure I had much choice. Where's Tanglefoot?"

"In there." Sharpe nodded toward the inner cells. "What's this about him being the wrong man?"

"Just that. He didn't do it."

"He was on the mine grounds," the deputy said.

"Looking for me, probably."

"You know, that's what he said," Sharpe, puzzled, told him.

"But you wouldn't listen."

"You can't give any credence to an Indian's word."

"No," Justice said bitterly.

"Tanglefoot?" Jody shook his head doubtfully. "He don't know what the truth is."

"Let's talk to him," Justice suggested.

"All right." Jody looked to the other deputies. "Keep it buttoned up. No one else gets in." To Ruff he said, "I don't see what good it can do to talk to Tanglefoot."

"None, unless you want to straighten this thing out," Ruff Justice shot back.

"You don't think much of me, do you?" Jody asked.

"What do you care what I think? Do your job. Let's talk to the Ute."

"He'll only lie."

"But I won't."

Jody hesitated again. He had the key to the cell-block door in his hand. "You really know who did it?" he asked.

"I know."

"Tell me, then," the deputy said.

"After we talk to Tanglefoot. You're going to have a hard-enough time accepting it as it is."

Ty Roosevelt called out, "They're coming up the steps now, Jody!"

"Keep 'em back. If they get any closer, fire a warning shot out the loophole. Over their heads."

Jody turned and opened the iron door behind them. Entering the narrow corridor, Ruff saw the figure of a dejected Tanglefoot sitting on the edge of an iron bunk. His eyes brightened a little when he saw Justice.

"Hello, tall man."

"Hello, Tanglefoot."

"What are you doing here?" the Ute asked.

"I've come to get you out." Jody scowled at Ruff's answer, and he backed away slightly, as if fearing a jail-break attempt.

"I went to the mine to look for you. I saw the person you were waiting for go up to the Never-Never tonight. On the hill above the shaft."

"Did he tell you this?" Ruff asked Jody.

"Yeah, but—"

"It's true. He was watching the mine for me. I hired him on. He was an employee of the Never-Never as far as I'm concerned, and he damn sure will never be prosecuted for anything as long as Katie Price is the owner." He waited for an answer to his unasked question.

Jody told him quietly, "She's all right, Justice. Sitting up and sipping oyster stew the last report I got."

Ruff let out a breath he had been holding without realizing it. "Fine, now what do you say we get all of this straightened out and quick."

"I'd like nothing better; if—"

From the outer office a rifle boomed. Ty Roosevelt had fired through the narrow loophole beside the door, aiming over the heads of the mob. They could hear and feel the building shake as the miners beat a hasty retreat down the stairs.

"If," Jody Sharpe continued a little shakily, "you will just tell me who the hell we are looking for, just who it is that's been causing all of this bloody hell!"

And Ruff told him.

15

"You're joking," Sharpe repeated. "That little wisp of a thing."

"It's no joke. It's Lily Sly we want, and from what Tanglefoot has told us, she's out at the Never-Never right now."

"Trying to do what?"

"To blow it up. Look, I don't have time to go through all that's happened, all of my reasons, but believe me, she's behind everything. She killed Les Coyle, and she tried to kill Katie Price. Let's bring her in—you talk to her. I've got a feeling that she would crack pretty easily if the pressure were put on. She's pretty unstable, Jody. I noticed it before, but I thought she was just reacting to the loss of Les Coyle. Now I can look back and see that it was more than that."

"She's crazy?"

"As a loon."

From the office Ty called out again. "Jody, they're coming back."

"We'll do it your way. I have to accept your word on this," Sharpe told Ruff.

"You'll go to the mine with me, let Tanglefoot out?"

"Sure," the deputy said tightly, "if you can figure out how to get us out of here."

As he said that, another shot was fired, but this one came from the outside. Jody let Tanglefoot out of the cell, and the three men went into the office, Ty Roosevelt casting a dark and doubtful glance at the Ute.

"What's up?" Ty asked.

"Mister Justice is going to settle the mob down for us," Sharpe said with irony.

"He is, is he? How?"

"He hasn't confided in me. But he's going to try, aren't you, Justice?"

"I'm going to try." Ruff unbuckled his gun belt and handed it to Jody Sharpe, who took it without comment.

"And what happens if you fail?"

"Then, Deputy, you're going to have to lower your sights a little. You'll have to start killing some miners." Ruff nodded, lifted the bar on the door, and stepped out into the torchlit night.

They were a dark and angry thing prowling the night. As Ruff stepped out, a sound like a deep growl met his ears. He could feel their anger, their need to hurt, wash over him.

"Who the hell is that?"

"Who are you? Wait, it's that Justice fellah."

"Get out of the way, Justice. We got us a rope and we have a man to kill."

Justice waited for them to quiet a little. Then he spoke. "He's the wrong one, men."

"What do you mean he's the wrong one? Are you

crazy? Every one knows it's the Ute that done the flooding, that killed three of us."

"Everyone's wrong." Ruff held up a hand. He decided to stretch things a little. "I'll tell you something that might surprise you. Tanglefoot was hired by the Never-Never to help catch the real killer. He was up there tonight working on this case."

"You're a damned liar, Justice! What kind of story is that?"

"You just want to get the man off."

"Take it easy," Justice said, holding up his hands. "Just because you built that gallows out there doesn't mean you have to use it."

"We'll use it, all right. Damn it all, get out of my way," a huge man in a torn red shirt said. "Or I'll tear you apart."

"Not likely, Kevin. That's the man that whipped Blue Boy Weaver."

Kevin, whoever he was, paused and blinked. He wasn't going to let something like that stop him, but it gave him something to think about.

"I don't give a damn," he said at last. He couldn't back down in front of the others. He wanted some of Justice, and he stepped up onto the landing to face him. "He's lyin', lyin' while they try to figure out some way to save the Ute's skin."

"I'm telling you the truth," Justice said—even if the truth was being tugged out of shape a little—"Tanglefoot worked for mine security."

"I don't believe you," Kevin said.

A voice from below asked, "Would you believe me, Rollins?"

Nathan Burbank was there in his dark suit and dark hat, hands in his pockets. He walked up the steps, the miners parting for their boss.

"I heard you men were trying to get each other hurt. That's not much good for the Never-Never, Rollins."

"Mister Burbank . . ."

"What happens when the deputies up there have to start shooting? You think those bullets are going to bounce off you, Kev? My first shift will be short a lead man tomorrow, won't it?"

"That Ute killed—"

"That Ute," Burbank said, "is working for security. It seemed smart to keep that fact secret. Now you know. The rest of you, do you hear me? Justice is telling you the truth. If you want some proof, how about this?" He unfolded a blue voucher of some kind and held it over his head. "This is Tanglefoot's paycheck! You think I'm paying a man who doesn't work for me, tight as I am with the owner's cash?"

That worked, it got a laugh. Burbank tucked the voucher away. "Tonight I'll spend some cash. Not the mine's, but my own. I'm buying drinks for you all. Not at one of those Delaney Street dives either. Let's try the Grand Hotel's bar and find out if that bonded whiskey is all they say it is."

That brought another cheer. Burbank should have been a politician. The miners started down the steps, laughing, talking loudly, arms slung over one another's shoulders. Burbank gave Kevin a half-dozen gold pieces. "Make good my promise, all right, Rollins? Don't try that bonded too often, though. I need you at five-thirty in the morning."

"All right, Mister Burbank, sure. Justice . . . sorry."

Ruff took the big callused hand. "No hard feelings. You couldn't have known."

"You really have the other one—the real killer?" Kevin asked.

"We've got the killer," Justice said. Burbanks' eyes

168

narrowed. "And we'll see that justice is done. I'd tear down that gallows if I were you."

"Sure," the man said a little shamefaced. Then, looking at the gold pieces in his hand, he ambled away. At the foot of the steps stood Hank Ryker, looking constrained in a town suit, and slightly puzzled.

"Everything all right?" he asked, climbing the stairs.

"Now," Justice said. "Thanks to your boss. That was a nice piece of work, Burbank. I appreciate it."

"Those are my people. I don't want them hurt."

"I'd like to see Tanglefoot's bank draft sometime, though, see if he could cash that in town."

Burbank smiled faintly. "Only if he wanted to pick up my shirts at the Chinese laundry. I noticed one day they had receipts the same color as our vouchers. Don't know what made it pop into my head just now."

"Glad it did. I'll let you know how this turns out."

"No you won't," Burbank said. "You say you know where the killer is."

"At the Never-Never, I think."

"That does it. We're going with you."

"You are, are you?"

"That's right. It's settled. Or we go alone."

"Could you shoot a woman?" Justice asked.

"What are you saying? The killer is a woman?"

"That's right."

Burbank glanced at Ryker, who looked worried. Then the mine boss answered, "If she's killed my people, I guess I could do it. If I had to. If you're sure."

"Oh, I'm sure," Ruff told them, "damned sure. Though in a way I wish I weren't." He shook his head and walked into the office as Jody opened the door and peered out cautiously.

The deputy didn't like it, but they all went along to the mine, riding swiftly and silently through the night. Ruff and Tanglefoot, Burbank and Ryker, Jody Sharpe and Ty Roosevelt.

There was no talking. Each man kept his own company, thought his own thoughts. Ruff was haunted by one particular memory. The woman, blond and fair, girlish and yet mature in her sexuality, came from out of the darkness to stand before the fire, choosing to lay down with him, to hold him and make love to him, while outside the thunder rumbled, and she shivered in his arms, a small, confused thing.

A twisted thing.

The mine was dark. Around the perimeters, guards still stood watch, for all the good they had done. But then which of them was going to suspect a petite little blonde of anything, even if Lily were seen! Who would suspect her of being more than she appeared to be—beautiful, young, wistful—until she tried to bash in your head for you?

They rode on through the gate, the guards, recognizing Ryker and Burbank, standing aside as they proceeded to the mine office, where they swung down in unison.

"How are we going to do this?" Jody asked Ruff.

"First of all, we'd better seal off all the exits. I've seen the map of this mine, and there's half a dozen ways out from Number Two."

"If she knows them."

"You can bet she does. This mine has been her obsession for a long while."

"How do you know she's here?" Burbank asked. He was interrupted by a man with the answer. His name was Ned, and he was one of the perimeter guards. He ran up, panting, rifle in hands, hatless and excited.

"Mister Burbank, how'd you know?"

"Know what?"

"Hiram Studdard—he was walking the fence down near the tailings dump . . . Mister Burbank," the man said, swallowing hard, "someone's killed him."

Burbank looked grimly at Ryker and then at Justice. "Let's go. Ned, call all the guards in. Seal off the Never-Never. We're looking for a woman."

"A woman, but, Mister Burbank—"

"Get moving, Ned!"

"Yes, sir."

"What do we do, Justice?" Jody asked, "I want to go with you."

"You and Ty watch the entrance to the main shaft. I'm going down into Number Two."

"Why worry about it? She can't get out."

"I'm worried," Justice said, "about what she's doing while she's down there. She's tried to blow the mountain up before. It wouldn't surprise me if she's got a dynamite charge with her."

Jody seemed a bit less reluctant to go down with Justice, but Ryker was stripping off his coat.

"You don't need to do this, Ryker."

"I know the place better than she does, better than anyone does. Besides," he said, lifting his eyes to the mountain, "she's part mine. I dug a lot of her. I want to try to save the old lady."

Ryker snatched up a lantern, and he and Justice started for the entrance to Number Two, the others following along at a rapid trot. The gate and perimeter guards were running toward the Never-Never now, coming to seal it off. But Ruff hardly saw them. His eyes were focused on the black mouth of the mine, this haunted, troubling place.

Tanglefoot, who had been silent, following but offering nothing, halted dead at the entrance of the mine. Ruff didn't blame him. Who would voluntarily go into the dark world of the earth spirits, into that bad-luck mine?

Except the mad ones.

Ruff plunged on, Ryker on his heels. Their lantern danced crazily on the walls of the cavern as they ran toward the down shaft. Somewhere below a madwoman was working, perhaps cackling, biting her lips with glee, her eyes bright as she struck a match and touched it to a hissing, serpentine fuse.

It wasn't a cheering picture.

They reached the bucket, and Ryker panted. "We both can't go. I'll winch you down, then I'll check along the upper stope. Take the lantern. There's half a dozen in the box over there."

Justice was in the bucket, his feet settling only a fraction of a second before Ryker, shoulders bulging, began to lower him. He swung through the darkness, descending much faster than on the previous trip. How had the woman gotten to the second level if she was down there? Of course there were other ways in, more circuitous, but that would have suited her better than marching through the main-shaft opening.

The bucket jarred the earth and shook those concerns out of Ruff's mind. She was here, that was all that mattered. He knew she was here because she had killed again to reach the mine. She would be in Number Two because that was the rich one, the one that straddled the vein of pure gold six feet wide.

Justice blew out his lantern and crouched in the darkness, the all-encompassing darkness. He wanted to be able to hear, to be able to detect any intimation of light, to feel the warmth of another human body.

He crept on now, moving with extreme caution. He knew the mine a little, but most of what he had learned had been on paper, and the touch of hard rock, the smell of the mine, the tiny gusts of wind with no apparent source, cool and swirling, were all impossible to draw with a pen.

He followed the iron rails, sliding his boot along the polished surface of one of them. The rails would lead to the gold. Would she be there as well? Drawn by it irresistibly?

Ruff stopped and blinked. He thought he had seen a light. The palest hint of light up a side shaft. Now it was gone. There was only the darkness. He moved on, uncertain now, not knowing if he had missed an opportunity or if his eyes had been playing tricks on him.

The inside of his boot still slid along the rail, guiding him into the depths of Number Two, the silent depths where nothing lived, could ever live, but only died.

He heard sounds now where none had been before— the slow trickling of water; the scuttling of tiny creatures; the sloughing off of rock and gravel, loosened by the day's digging, surrendering to gravity.

And then the other sound. Faintly metallic, very distant seemingly, yet near at hand.

Justice turned and started back toward the side shaft where he had seen the light, because she was there. She was there with her mad ideas and her deadly intent and her beautiful body and her black, black heart.

He ran his hand along the wall of the shaft, and when it touched nothing but air, he turned into the shaft, his bowie in hand because now he wasn't dealing with a woman, but with one of the dark things, one of the tormented, one of the deadly.

He saw the faintest glow of light against the wall of the shaft ahead of him, and his heart lifted with excitement, his groin tightened, and his mouth went dry. He moved silently forward, creeping toward the point of light. She had to have her lantern masked somehow, probably using black tape so that she was provided with only a pencil-thin beam of light, enough to see by, enough to set a charge by.

Then he rounded the elbow in the shaft and found her.

16

She was in a man's shirt and jeans, crouched over a bundle of dynamite. At the sound of Ruff's footstep she spun, and before he could grab her, she had leapt back to stand panting against the wall of the cave, her blond hair falling across her eyes, her hands holding a cocked .44 revolver, which she was aiming directly at Ruff's belly.

"This is no good, Lily," he said softly.

"I thought you liked me."

"I do."

Her voice was childish, singsong. "No you don't. I thought you did, but then I found out the truth. If you liked me, you wouldn't have been trying to hunt me down all this time."

"I didn't know it was you."

She never heard him. "If you liked me, you wouldn't have slept with Katie. I found out about that. A servant said something. So I knew. Why do the men always go to her?"

"Like the Duke?" Ruff was trying to ease closer, but

she was watching him like a cat watches a mouse, the big bore of that Colt following Justice.

"The Duke, yes. I had to kill him. He wouldn't pay any attention to me."

"Les paid attention to you, plenty of it."

"Oh, Les," she said disparagingly. "A lawman. What did he have? He didn't have any money. He was just nothing, but I had to keep an eye on him. He got too close a number of times. I think in the end he would have found out. So I had to kill him."

"You picked a risky time."

"Did I?" She bit her lip thoughtfully and then shook her head. "No, that was a good time. Who would suspect me at my own engagement party? If I lost control, they would blame it on shock and grief. Besides, I was hoping they'd think someone meant to kill you. And they did for a while, didn't they?"

"Some of them," Ruff answered.

"It was fortunate that Chase Longden sent Campbell around to bully Les that night. That put the blame on Campbell, didn't it?"

"Who killed Campbell?"

"Why, I did," she said with surprise. "That was clever too, wasn't it? I saw him. I knew who it was. Then, when they put me in my room to lie down, to rest, I went out the window. While you were busy searching the grounds, I went to Longden's, up the back stairs, and to Campbell's room. I finished him, and it should have finished your investigation. But you had to keep looking!" Her voice had risen to a shriek. Her hands trembled and Ruff was afraid she was going to jerk off a shot purely by accident. He took another cautious step toward her.

"You know there's gas down here, don't you, Lily? Can't you smell it? If you fire that gun, you're liable to spark an explosion."

"You're making that up."

"Even a match could do it—the fuse."

"Stay back, Justice. I don't believe you."

"I'm telling you the truth."

"One more step and I'll kill you," she said, and coming from Lily Sly, it was more than an idle threat. Ruff halted.

"I'm not making that up about the gas. It's very strong in this shaft. There's no ventilation at all back here. The whole place could go up, you included."

"I don't care if the whole place goes up! Why should I? It's Katie's."

"And yours."

She smiled craftily. "Not yet," she said in a small, sly voice. "But now that Katie's dead, I'll have everything she's got socked away, her house and her dresses, and when people come to Denver, they'll point at my house and talk about *me!*"

"Katie's not dead."

"Then . . ." She stopped abruptly and stared at Justice, her pretty head cocked like a pup's. "What do you mean?" she asked carefully.

"She didn't die."

"You're making this up too." She laughed a little raggedly, a little crazily. "I know she's dead. I got her from twenty feet away. With *this*." She showed Ruff the gun, as if it proved everything. "She's dead."

"No. Don't you see, Lily, it's all over now? You can't win. Katie's alive; she'll testify. Tanglefoot saw you. *I* know. Staggs talked."

She stood there reeling, touching her head as if it hurt her to think.

"All you can do is come in voluntarily, Lily. No jury is going to hang a woman, not in Colorado."

"Everything was perfect," she said in wonder.

"Not perfect. You slipped here and there. Now they know, everyone knows."

She looked at Justice, at him and through him with her blue-gray eyes, wide and innocent and cruel. "Well," she said at last, "there's only one thing left to do, then."

"Yes, that's right." He stretched out a hand. "Give me the gun and come along."

"No." She shook her head. "Not that. I mean the mine." She lifted her eyes to the Never-Never's dark walls. "That would teach Katie something, wouldn't it? *That* would show her that I was *someone*."

"Lily, you're not thinking right."

"Get back! Damm it, get back! I'm thinking straight, and I'm going to do it. It's that easy, is it? Just fire the gun?"

"Lily, please!"

"I don't even need the dynamite. Get back, Justice!" She smiled faintly, dreamily. "I'd like to have you kiss me once more, but you'd only grab for the gun. I'm very strong; I surprise people with my strength, but I couldn't fight you off."

"Lily . . ."

"I like you, Justice. I like you very much. I ought to shoot you for sleeping-with Katie, but I won't. You won't want her anymore after she's poor again, anyway. You felt sorry for me one night and helped me when the thunder was loud and the rain was pounding down, and so I'm going to let you live."

"Listen, Lily, all of this can be straightened out."

"Yes, I'm going to let you live. If you start now. If you go. Because . . ." She was panting heavily now, as if she couldn't breathe in the narrow side shaft.

Ruff made one more try at slipping closer, needing only another step, only three feet more to be able to lunge for the pistol, to have a chance. But Lily Sly was having none of it. Her eyes gleamed. The black wall behind her shone softly. In it Justice could see threads of gold, deadly gold, tracing primitive artwork, sketching secret words that only the mad could read.

"Lily . . ."

"I will count to twenty-five. When I reach that number, I will fire this pistol." Her voice was high, childish again.

"Lily, dammit!" Ruff could only grind his teeth together. How do you combat madness? He had stood up against guns and knives, war axes and hard weather. He hadn't come up against anything like this before, however, and he knew he didn't have the weapons to fight it. She was counting.

"Five . . . six . . . seven . . ."

"Justice?"

It was Ryker, and Ruff spun around at the sound of his voice. Ryker's eyes were wide with shock and apprehension. "Good God, if she touches off . . ."

"Get out of here, Ryker. She's going to shoot."

"Twelve . . . thirteen . . ."

"Justice!" Ryker said, his voice low now, jittery. "We've got to get out of here."

"Fifteen . . ."

"I've got to try to stop her," Ruff snapped.

"Before she can squeeze the trigger? You're dreaming. Come on! Now!"

Ruff looked to the desperate Ryker, then back to Lily, who was smiling as she held the gun up, pointing it at Ruff's face. She was far away, too far away.

"Good-bye, Lily," Justice said. "I'm sorry."

"Justice!" Ryker grabbed Ruff's arm and they made for the main shaft, Ryker with his lantern leading the way. There wasn't time to get out, there just wasn't. Ten seconds . . . unless Lily had been bluffing. If so, she should have been a poker player. She would have made her millions if she could bluff like that. Ruff wiped the sweat from his eyes, cold sweat he hadn't felt trickling down.

"We'll never get up in the bucket," Justice called out.

"This way—another opening. Straight down the hillside," Ryker puffed. "Ventilation."

Everything happened at once then, and even later Ruff could never get the sequence arranged precisely in his mind. There was a dark hole pasted against the darkness, a single star, shining from the vast, clean distances. Then there was an explosion, terrible and ear-crushing, shooting flame and dust everywhere, and Justice was falling through space, rock and sand washing over him. He saw Ryker go one way and his lantern another, until he himself smashed against the solid flank of the mountain, rolled another thirty or forty feet, and got up to run with Ryker into the darkness of the hillside forest, while explosion after explosion ripped through the Never-Never and the mad thing that had pulled the trigger was buried beneath the tons of rubble and pure, bright gold.

Then it was over and there was nothing left to do but stand and look at the smoke rising into the starry sky over Denver, knowing that nothing had been done to help Les Coyle, nothing to help the miners and their families, nothing to help a desolate, unhappy young woman with a strange set of values.

"We'll not dig that out easily," Ryker said. There was a gash across his cheek and he was bleeding pretty freely.

"Will it be worth it?" Ruff asked.

Ryker shrugged. "When they go down like that, you're not dealing with stable rock anymore. Maybe, for that much gold, they'll try it. I don't know." The miner was nostalgic. "She was a good piece of work."

It was a long hike in the darkness back to the front of the Never-Never. Half the town had come out to see what could be seen. It was little enough, a vast mound of rubble still smoking, now and then shifting. Ruff and Ryker found Burbank near the office, which still stood.

"We thought you two were inside," the mine boss said.

"Nearly," Ryker replied. "How's it look, boss?"

"It looks like a year's work," Burbank said gloomily.

"Was anyone hurt?" Ruff asked.

"Ned was blown off the ledge up there. Suffered some burns and a few bruises. The rest of us are all right. We heard the rumbling down below and took off. I felt it underfoot—I've seen them go before."

"Where's Tanglefoot?"

"Gone. Back to the hills. He was saying something I didn't get, something about dark spirits. Maybe you know what he meant."

"Yes," Ruff Justice said, "maybe I do."

Morning was bright and clear. When Ruff dressed, pulling on a white shirt and dark trousers, brushing back his long hair, the woman was standing in the door, leaning on a cane, watching.

"Christ, Katie, what are you doing on your feet? The doctor said—"

"Blast the doctor! Don't let them get you down, that's my theory. Once they get you down, you're in trouble. That's when the illnesses set in. Why, a woman's made to be up on her feet, not lying flat on her back in some bed"—she squinted at Ruff—"but then you wouldn't agree with that, would you?"

"No." Justice laughed and went to her. "Not precisely."

"Kiss me, you bastard, Justice," she said. "But not too hard. It might hurt."

"No, not this time, I promise." He kissed her gently and she looked up with her green eyes deeply lighted.

Ruff winked. "You've got to at least sit down," he told her.

"All right," Katie Price said, "at the breakfast table. Take me down and let's have our last breakfast in this monstrosity of a house."

"It's really lost?"

"The lawyers say so. Not officially yet, but they don't think I can win. It seems the Duke Duchamp-Villon was a bad boy. Française-Froebel is a huge corporation with a lot of lawyers, and they've evidently shown that the Duke had agreed not to act as his own agent while in their employ. His purchase of the mine was invalidated—or will be."

"I'm sorry, Katie."

"Oh, hell, I don't care much. I was tired of this life of leisure. I've still got some of my own money from the sale of the Scottish Wheel, and the lawyers say there will undoubtedly be some sort of settlement given me for the mine, so . . ." She shrugged.

"All gone," Ruff said. He was quiet for a minute and Katie knew what he was thinking.

"I know—if Lily had gotten everything she wanted, she would have lost it overnight to the corporation. All of it was for nothing, nothing at all."

"Murder usually is. It's a hell of an option for solving your problems. What are you going to do now, Katie?"

"Me?" She took his arm and they started downstairs, Ruff snatching up his hat and gun belt. He didn't think he'd be coming back to the big house again. "I've gotten along before. Blue Boy Weaver's place is for sale. I might just buy it, open up a new saloon. Call it the Denver Duchess. What do you think of that?"

"If it suits you, Katie."

She stopped, leaning against him. "It would suit me a lot better if you'd stay and help me out, Ruffin."

"Can't, Katie, you know that."

"The army?"

"That's right—they're missing a scout."

"No." She shook her head. "it's not the army that takes you away from me. It's something else, a need to wander, to find . . . Just what it is you're trying to find, Justice? What is it that makes men like you what they are?"

"Dark spirits," he said enigmatically, and then he kissed her again, lightly.

"That one," she said, "hurt just a little."

"Come on," Ruff Justice said, "let's get on down to the banquet. The last banquet."

The man suddenly leapt out of the empty room to their right, and before Justice had time to react, Angel Farmer had put two rounds through his revolver. Both missed, but Katie Price screamed and slumped to the ground as Justice, pawing at his holster, came up with his long-barreled Colt.

The big gun bucked twice in his hand, the second shot echoing through the house just as Angel Farmer's third bullet slammed into the wall, chewing out a chunk of plaster and spraying Justice with fine powder.

But Farmer had been too angry, too anxious, and he had missed again. Ruff's bullets hadn't missed. The rapist took both of them in the chest and staggered forward, his mouth spewing blood, his eyes white and crazed, stretching out an empty hand toward Ruff Justice before he toppled forward on his face and lay there dead.

Ruff turned to Katie. She was slow in getting up even with his help. She leaned against the wall, panting, holding her breast.

"That's why I'll miss you, Ruff Justice. You do liven up a house. Come on now." She took his arm. "Let's have that last breakfast together."

WESTWARD HO!

The following is the opening section from the next novel in the gun-blazing, action-packed new Ruff Justice series from Signet:

RUFF JUSTICE #22: THE OPIUM QUEEN

1

There was a lot of blood in the streets of Denver, and some of it had been left there by the tall man with long dark hair and a mustache that drooped to his jawline. His name was Ruff Justice and he had seen trouble in this town.

He stood for a moment longer beneath the awning of the hotel, looking back up Delaney Street to where the lights blazed and the men were shouting, cursing, betting a month's wages on the spin of a wheel while they soaked their brains in raw whiskey. He had been in a place like that this evening, not because he liked the noise, the glare of lights, the threat of sudden violence, but because a very nice lady had just opened a new watering hole for Denver's thirsty men.

It was called the Denver Duchess, and she was called Katie Price, and once not so long ago she had been very wealthy. Not so long ago, too, she had slept with the tall man in buckskins, the man who now shook his head and turned his back on the hustle and bustle of Delaney Street, on the Denver Duchess, on Denver.

Ruff started into the hotel, but before he reached the black doors, a cry from the alley turned his head and his hand dropped to his Colt revolver. He went to the head of the alley, which was dank and dark, smelling of refuse and rot.

A big man with a huge belly and a long knife leapt out from behind the barrels. He was dressed in white silk with a crimson sash. His moon face showed tiny gleaming eyes. The knife slashed at Ruff Justice and the tall man jerked back, his eyes picking out the two struggling figures farther down the alley.

One of them was a woman, young, wearing a close-fitting dress without petticoats—Chinese. The other was also Oriental, smaller than the thug in front of Justice, but no gentler from the way he was handling the girl.

"You, no you business. Go away," the Chinese with the knife said.

"It is my business." Ruff showed him the Colt, and the man with the knife shook his head heavily.

"No you business. Just a bad girl. Just a bad girl," the round man said.

"Mister, get out of my way. Or try it with that knife— but I don't think you'll have much luck with it. A bullet's a hell of a lot faster."

"No, no you business—"

The Colt spat flame, and a bullet at the Chinese thug's feet sprayed him with alley gravel. The man stood for a minute, glaring at Ruff with pure hatred.

"Maybe you die, tall man," he said.

"Maybe so. That shot's going to bring some curious people, mister. Maybe the law, too—you know the law in Denver?"

"I know . . ." The Chinese started backing away up the alley, and Justice followed him, prodding him back. The second man stood motionless over the girl on the ground. She was in white, one leg drawn up to show a delicate knee through a torn seam.

Both men moved away as Justice came nearer.

"Are you all right?" he asked the girl.

She had her glossy dark hair done elaborately into four braids that wound around the formed loops. There was a tortoiseshell comb in her hair at the wrong angle. The eyes Ruff was looking into were huge, almond-shaped. "Are you all right?" he repeated.

"She don't speak English," the fat man said again. "No speaking from her. Just a bad girl. This man's daughter. We take away."

"Touch her and I'll blow your hand off. You two scat, now," Ruff suggested. The Colt emphasized his request.

"She no speak, mister."

"Then I'll find someone to speak for her. Someone that won't lie. Get." The muzzle of the Colt raised. "The next one won't be in the dirt, my friend."

The two of them conversed heatedly in rapid Chinese. Then they backed away still more, repeating the threat. "Maybe you die, tall man. Maybe you die."

Ruff put a bullet past the man's head and they took to their heels. Justice watched the head of the alley for a long while, and when he was sure they had gone for good, he holstered his gun and returned his attention to the young Chinese girl, who hadn't moved an inch in all that while.

She wasn't over twenty. Pert, pointed breasts thrust at the white silk of her dress. Her hips were lean and tightly encased in the dress, except where it had split open from the bullying she had taken. There Ruff saw a patch of smooth golden flesh. Long legs tapered down to extremely tiny feet, which might have been bound when she was younger, as was the custom of her people, who had a cultural fetish for small feet.

"They're gone. Do you understand English at all?" Justice asked.

"Li Po, Li Po," she said excitedly. Ruff didn't know if it was her name, a cry for help, or something to eat.

"Right. Can you stand up? Get up now." He motioned with his hands and she sat up, tucking her legs under her. She looked woozy sitting there, bracing herself with her hands. She simply stared at him.

"Come on, those friends of yours might be back. Get up, all right?"

And then simultaneously Justice noticed the dreaminess in the girl's eyes and smelled the sweet, somehow familiar scent that drifted onto Delaney Street from the Chinese quarter.

The girl was floating along on an opium cloud. Maybe she didn't even know where she was, what was happening.

He crouched down and looked more closely into her eyes. "Dammit, woman, I can't leave you here. Get up, will you?"

There was still no answer. Ruff put an arm around her, hefted and slung her over his shoulder. He put his hand on the back of her thigh to steady her, feeling the lithe muscle beneath the silk. The girl giggled.

"Shut up," he growled.

He had to be leaving Denver. He was supposed to be in Dakota. The army was expecting him back. Colonel MacEnroe, the commander at Fort Lincoln, Dakota Territory, would be having a fit. Ruff's "temporary" absence was turning into a career in Colorado.

Now, this.

The smart thing to do would be to walk her over to the jailhouse on Bond Street and dump her in Jody Sharpe's lap. But the acting marshal of Denver was on an antiopium crusade just now, and it had turned into an anti-Chinese jihad. Ruff didn't know the girl, but he didn't want to see her locked up or deported.

"Come on," he grumbled as if she had a choice, slung over his shoulder like that. He walked around the corner and through the black doors of the hotel, past the desk clerk—who goggled but knew enough about men not to say anything—and upstairs to his small, cold room, where his war sack rested in the corner, along with his rifle, a .56 Spencer in its buckskin sheath with the Crow beadwork.

Ruff dumped the girl on his bed.

"Li Po," she said.

"Yeah." He crossed to the window and opened it, looking out at Denver for a minute before glancing back at the girl. "Now I have a problem—you're it. I was getting ready to leave tonight. I've got a long way to go. If I could catch the train, I could save myself a lot of riding."

She nodded, listening intently, understanding none of it. She was pretty, very pretty, by lamplight.

"Because of you, I'm liable to miss my train. I couldn't

leave you out in the street, but I can't leave you here either. My rent's up tonight. They'll toss you back out in the street. I could pay for the room, but who knows if you'd stay—or if they haven't watched us, waiting for a chance to come after you. I wish I knew what you'd done, who you were. Don't you speak any English at all?"

Her eyes brightened. "Ham and eggs!"

"Fine." Ruff looked heavenward. "Hungry?" He made eating motions and she nodded. "All right, I'll see if I can find someone to cook you something. Ham and eggs, huh?"

She nodded again, so energetically that Ruff had to smile. So she did speak English—after a fashion. Someone had taught her enough so that she could order breakfast in a strange land.

Justice opened the door a little, and when a bellboy came past, he gave him an order for the kitchen and a silver dollar. He turned back to the girl, closing the door. "He'll get ham and eggs, all right?"

And she said prettily, "Prease."

"Yeah, *prease*. Now what do I do with you, woman?"

Ruff turned the chair beside the window and sat watching the girl. She hadn't been in Denver long, but someone had brought her, taught her one phrase, filled her up with opium, and put her on the streets to be beat up by fat men.

"And what business is it of mine? Your friend was right, you know. No my business."

The girl nodded, smiling deeply, distantly. She was floating away into lotus land, her expression glazed and empty. Justice damn near left her, just locked the door and left, but the second time he went to the window he saw them. The fat man was down below. That white suit of his stood out in the darkness like a beacon. They were waiting, watching. They knew.

When the bellboy brought the ham and eggs, Ruff had to nudge the girl awake to eat. Once started, she ate with an appetite that was nearly incredible, shoving the food in, her white teeth and pretty pink tongue making short work of it all.

When there was nothing left on the tray, she gave it to Justice and leaned back on his bed, smiling up at him, hands folded over her belly.

"Any good?" Ruff asked dryly. But she didn't answer. He walked to the window, placed the tray on the table, and yanked the blind down angrily. "If only you could speak English, just a little more English," he said.

When he turned back toward the bed, she was lying there naked, smiling up at him, her arms stretched out.

"Prease pay in advance," was what she said.

SIGNET Brand Westerns You'll Enjoy

(0451)

- [ ] LUKE SUTTON: OUTLAW by Leo P. Kelley. (115228—$1.95)*
- [ ] LUKE SUTTON: GUNFIGHTER by Leo P. Kelley. (122836—$2.25)*
- [ ] LUKE SUTTON: INDIAN FIGHTER by Leo P. Kelley. (124553—$2.25)*
- [ ] LUKE SUTTON: AVENGER by Leo P. Kelley. (128796—$2.25)*
- [ ] AMBUSCADE by Frank O'Rourke. (094905—$1.75)*
- [ ] BANDOLEER CROSSING by Frank O'Rourke. (111370—$1.75)
- [ ] THE BIG FIFTY by Frank O'Rourke. (111419—$1.75)
- [ ] THE BRAVADOS by Frank O'Rourke. (114663—$1.95)*
- [ ] THE LAST CHANCE by Frank O'Rourke. (115643—$1.95)*
- [ ] LATIGO by Frank O'Rourke. (111362—$1.75)
- [ ] THE PROFESSIONALS by Frank O'Rourke. (113527—$1.95)*
- [ ] SEGUNDO by Frank O'Rourke. (117816—$2.25)*
- [ ] VIOLENCE AT SUNDOWN by Frank O'Rourke. (111346—$1.95)
- [ ] COLD RIVER by William Judson. (123085—$2.50)
- [ ] THE HALF-BREED by Mick Clumpner. (112814—$1.95)*
- [ ] MASSACRE AT THE GORGE by Mick Clumpner. (117433—$1.95)*
- [ ] BROKEN LANCE by Frank Gruber. (113535—$1.95)*
- [ ] QUANTRELL'S RAIDERS by Frank Gruber. (097351—$1.95)*
- [ ] TOWN TAMER by Frank Gruber. (110838—$1.95)*

*Prices slightly higher in Canada

**Buy them at your local
bookstore or use coupon
on next page for ordering.**

Ⱥ

Exciting SIGNET Westerns by Ernest Haycox

(0451)
- [ ] BUGLES IN THE AFTERNOON (114671—$2.25)*
- [ ] CHAFEE OF ROARING HORSE (114248—$1.95)*
- [ ] TRAIL SMOKE (112822—$1.95)*
- [ ] TRAIL TOWN (097793—$1.95)*
- [ ] CANYON PASSAGE (117824—$2.25)*
- [ ] DEEP WEST (118839—$2.25)*
- [ ] FREE GRASS (118383—$2.25)*
- [ ] HEAD OF THE MOUNTAIN (120817—$2.50)*
- [ ] SIGNET DOUBLE WESTERN: ACTION BY NIGHT and TROUBLE SHOOTER (130626—$3.50)*
- [ ] SIGNET DOUBLE WESTERN: THE BORDER TRUMPET and THE WILD BUNCH (131568—$3.50)*
- [ ] SIGNET DOUBLE WESTERN: SADDLE & RIDE and THE FEUDISTS (094670—$1.95)*
- [ ] SIGNET DOUBLE WESTERN: ALDER GULCH and A RIDER OF THE HIGH MESA (122844—$3.50)*

*Prices slightly higher in Canada

Buy them at your local bookstore or use this handy coupon for ordering:

NEW AMERICAN LIBRARY,
P.O. Box 999, Bergenfield, New Jersey 07621

Please send me the books I have checked above. I am enclosing $_____
(please add $1.00 to this order to cover postage and handling). Send check
or money order—no cash or C.O.D.'s. Prices and numbers are subject to change
without notice.

Name _____

Address_____

City_____ State_____ Zip Code_____
Allow 4-6 weeks for delivery.
This offer is subject to withdrawal without notice.